Cast of Characters

Henry Augustus Rudolfo Cremond Cremond. The Earl of Ornum, who takes his lordly responsibilities

Lady Millicent. His wife, the Countess, a pretty, rather vacant woman.

Lady Eleanor. Their daughter, a young woman of great common sense.

Lord Cremond. Henry, the Earl's son and heir, the image of his father.

William Murton. The Earl's blacksheep nephew, whose mother married a groom. He's a painter of modest success and a notorious sponger.

Miles Cremond. Another nephew, second in succession to the title.

Laura Cremond. His sharp-tongued wife.

Lady Alice and Lady Maud. The Earl's elderly, eccentric aunts.

Charles Purvis. The Earl's capable steward, who pines for Lady Eleanor.

Osborne Meredith. The Earl's dedicated librarian and archivist.

Walter Ames. The vicar, an expert on ancient weaponry and armor.

Dillow. The butler, a man of great presence.

Mrs. Morley. The housekeeper, a dependable woman

Detective Inspector C.D. Sloan. He's in charge of the investigation.

Detective Constable Crosby. A conscientious but literal-minded sort who is never Sloan's first choice as an assistant.

Superintendent Leeyes. Sloan's repressive superior, who'd much rather be dealing with problems in the traffic division.

Cromwell T. Fortescue. The head of the Young Masters Art Society.

Robert Hamilton. The county archivist.

Plus assorted servants, relatives, tour guides, tourists, police officials, members of the press, and a lone solicitor.

Books by Catherine Aird

(all featuring Inspector Sloan with the exception of
A Most Contagious Game)

The Religious Body* (1966)
A Most Contagious Game* (1967)
Henrietta Who?* (1968)
The Complete Steel (1969)
(*The Stately Home Murder** in the U.S.)
A Late Phoenix (1970)
His Burial Too (1973)
Slight Mourning (1975)
Parting Breath (1977)
Some Die Eloquent (1979)
Passing Strange (1980)
Last Respects (1982)
Harm's Way (1984)
A Dead Liberty (1986)
The Body Politic (1990)
A Going Concern (1993)
Injury Time (1994, short stories
featuring Sloan and others)
After Effects (1996)
Stiff News (1998)
Little Knell (2001)
Amendment Of Life (2003)
Chapter And Hearse (2004 , short stories
featuring Sloan and others)
A Hole in One (2005)
Losing Ground (2008)

*Reprinted by The Rue Morgue Press
as of July 2008

The Stately Home Murder

BY CATHERINE AIRD

Boulder / Lyons
Rue Morgue Press

About Catherine Aird

Catherine Aird's fourth book, *The Stately Home Murder* (first published in the United Kingdom in 1969 as *The Complete Steel*), features, as does all but one of her other novels, Inspector C.D. Sloan of the Calleshire C.I.D. You won't find Calleshire in any atlas. Like Anthony Trollope (followed by Angela Thirkell) and later Thomas Hardy, Aird chose to create an imaginary shire in which to set her stories, partly "so that it could have all the usual institutions without my having to worry about upsetting real people." Calleshire, however, no doubt in many ways resembles Kent, where Catherine Aird, a pseudonym for Kinn Hamilton McIntosh, born in Yorkshire in 1930, has made her home in a small village near Canterbury for most of her life, living in the same house since 1946. "Real life (and) that intimate knowledge of the same English village" has provided Aird with most of the background needed for her books. She suspects that her fellow villagers rarely think of her as a writer and are more likely to refer to her as the village doctor's daughter, a onetime golfer, and as an editor and publisher of village histories. She neglects to add that her neighbors might also have noticed that she was made an M.B.E. for her longtime work with the Girl Guides Association.

Some English critics, T.J. Binyon, for example, have grumbled that "it is difficult to create a sense of place with an imaginary locality" while grudgingly admitting that her books are "nicely contrived and pleasantly unpretentious." What Binyon fails to understand is that the majority of mystery readers, especially Americans, are more interested in a somewhat idealized English landscape than in the frequently blighted real thing.

Aird did not start out to be a writer. She intended to follow in her father's footsteps and study medicine but had to abandon that idea when she came down with nephrotic syndrome, a very serious condition that often leads to kidney failure. It's less lethal today, thanks to steroids and transplants, but more than a half century ago it forced her to take to bed for an extended period, during which she read a great deal of detective fiction, including Sapper, the Saint, Raymond Chandler, and, of course, one of her personal favorites, Josephine Tey, whose own *Daughter of*

Time also explores an historical mystery with the detective having to resort to research to solve a long-ago crime. Later she wrote "two or three bad novels before turning to crime so to speak—definitely a case of poacher turned gamekeeper."

Grounded as she was in the traditional mystery, it's not surprising that her books reflect many of the aspects of mysteries from the Golden Age of detection (roughly 1913 to 1953) when fair play was the name of the game and the reader an active participant in uncovering whodunit. Such a reader was Aird's mother, who would faithfully read the first couple of chapters of her daughter's manuscripts, jot down the name of the villain and then place this piece of paper in a sealed envelope to be opened when the book was done. Her mother figured out the villain every time. "Fine words, carefully crafted by me to conceal the murderer among a welter of more suspicious characters, buttered no parsnips with her," writes Aird.

Aird's entry into the ranks of crime writers was warmly welcomed by the critics. Crime fiction historian Melvyn Barnes cited her as one of the writers who "has breathed new life into the genre, concentrating mainly upon the cosy village puzzle of the golden age tradition but showing welcome unwillingness to maintain the rather colorless, unconvincing and formulaic approach of so many of her predecessors...those who say that the modern crime novel heralded the demise of the traditional mystery story will continue to be confounded by writers of Catherine Aird's standard." Her third book—and second Sloan—*Henrietta Who?* (1968) was picked by *New York Times* reviewer Allen J. Hubin as one of the best books of the year. In discussing her work in the *St. James Guide to Crime and Mystery Writers*, Pearl G. Aldrich said Aird was a throwback to "the leisurely, kinder, gentler crime novel.," displaying a tone that "is smiling, good-natured, good-mannered, (and) amusing." Aldrich points out that the "voice of the omniscient author is heard continuously, commenting, explaining, digressing, joking, adding extraneous information, and explaining English ways and attitudes." Aldrich is especially fond of *The Stately Home Murder*. Easily the funniest book in Aird's output, the action focuses on an eccentric titled family struggling to make ends meet. In 2002, this title was one of 103 mysteries chosen for inclusion in *They Died in Vain: Overlooked, Underappreciated and Forgotten Mystery Novels,* edited by Jim Huang with contributions from members of the Independent Mystery Booksellers Association.

For more information on Aird (and her one non-Sloan novel) see Tom & Enid Schantz' introduction to The Rue Morgue Press edition of *A Most Contagious Game*, from which this note on the author was excerpted.

"What may this mean,

That thou, dead corpse, again in complete steel
Revisit'st thus the glimpses of the moon ..."

Hamlet to Ghost

For Munro—or Ornum—with love

1

Ornum House was open to the public, which did not help the police one little bit.

On the contrary, in fact ...

It was open every Wednesday, Saturday, and Sunday from April to October, and to parties at other times by prior arrangement with the steward and comptroller.

It was also open—as all the guidebooks said—Bank Hols (Good Friday excepted). Henry Augustus Rudolfo Cremond Cremond, thirteenth Earl Ornum of Ornum in the County of Calleshire, drew the line at opening Ornum House on Good Friday.

"Religious holiday. Not a civil one. No beanfeasts in my house on Good Friday," he had decreed, adding, as he always added when the subject came up, "Don't know what m'father would have thought about having people in the house for money."

There was usually someone on hand to make a sympathetic noise at this point.

"Guests, family, and servants," his Lordship would go on plaintively. "That was all in his day. Now it's half Calleshire."

This understandable repugnance at having his family home tramped over did not, however, prevent him taking a close interest in the daily tally of visitors. At the end of every open day, Charles Purvis, his steward, was summoned to give an account of the numbers—much as in Scotland on the days succeeding the Glorious Twelfth of August, the gamekeeper presented himself each evening with the game bag totals.

Ornum House, attractive as it undoubtedly was, did not really compete in the Stately Home League Tables—it was too far off the beaten tourist track for that. Nevertheless it did have a respectable number of visitors each year. It was sufficiently near to Berebury to constitute a "must" for people coming to that town, and sufficiently far from the industrial complex of Luston to be an "outing" for people living there.

The outing was usually extended to cover visits to the thirteenth-century church of St. Aidan or the twentieth-century roadhouse The Fiddler's Delight—but seldom both.

On this particular Sunday in June the little church by the big house offered its own attractions. It was both quiet and cold and it was possible to sit down in a pew in peace and surreptitiously slip off shoes grown too small on a hot afternoon. It had the edge—temporarily, at least—on The Fiddler's Delight, which would not be open until six o'clock.

Mrs. Pearl Fisher was a member of the public who had come to see over Ornum House and her feet hurt.

She hadn't even got as far as the house itself yet and they hurt already. This was partly because they were crammed into her best pair of shoes and partly because she had spent too long standing on them. In the ordinary way she spent her Sunday afternoons having a quiet nap, but this Sunday was different.

Just how different it was going to be had not yet become apparent to Mrs. Fisher when she and the twins and the rest of their party spilled out of the coach just before lunchtime.

The house and grounds were both fuller than usual. It had been wet for three weekends in a row, and now, suddenly, it was flaming June with a vengeance. There had been picnickers all over the park since noon disporting themselves among the trees in a manner not envisaged by Capability Brown when invited to lay out the great park in the then modern manner. (That had been after one of the Earls of Ornum had clapped a Palladian front on the south side of the medieval house. And *that* had been after he had got back from his first Grand Tour.)

The public, though, seemed to have got the idea of Capability's pleasances. They were positively full of people taking conscious pleasure from walking in them, enjoying their alternating sun and shade and the smooth grass underfoot, and, every now and then, exclaiming at an unexpected vista carefully planned by that master craftsman for them to exclaim at.

At least two people had entered into the spirit of the folly, which was set on a little rise some way from the house.

"No," said Miss Mavis Palmer.

"Go on," urged her ardent young man.

"No," said Mavis, less firmly.

"Be a sport."

Mavis giggled.

They had come to Ornum House for the day with a coach party from Luston, and there was no question but that they were enjoying themselves.

Mrs. Pearl Fisher, who had come on the same coach, wasn't quite so sure she was. Apart from her feet, which were troubling her more than a little, there were the twins, Michael and Maureen, whom she had brought with her for the ample reason that Mr. Fisher would never have forgiven her for leaving them at home. *His* Sunday was sacrosanct to The King's Arms and his own armchair.

Like Miss Mavis Palmer and her young man, Bernard, she came from Paradise Row, Luston. Any student of industrial philanthropy would immediately recognize this as a particularly grimy part of that particularly grimy town. By some Victorian quirk of self-righteousness the street names there varied in inverse proportion to their amenity.

The coach had been booked from door to door—which was one of the reasons why Mrs. Fisher had put her best shoes on. What she had not reckoned with was the distance within the doors. There was no distance to speak of inside the house in Paradise Row, Luston, but there was a great deal of it once through the portals of Ornum House.

It had been an old house by the time Capability Brown saw it, and now it was an architectural nightmare. It was true to no one period, representational of nothing but a series of improvements by a series of owners. Behind the Palladian south front were Tudor bricks and behind those the remains of a donjon—a reminder that before the house there had been a castle with a great central keep.

Lord Ornum himself never forgot this.

"Those were the days," he would sigh. "Drawbridge, portcullis, and broadsword in that order and you were all right. Keep all your enemies at bay. But now"—here he would open his hands expressively—"now to keep out the enemy"—(he was referring to Her Majesty's Commissioners of Inland Revenue)—"I have to lower the drawbridge and let everyone else in."

Mrs. Pearl Fisher and the twins didn't join the other picnickers in the park.

They had their sandwiches near the little church that was not far from the house. Churches were something that the utterly urban Mrs. Fisher understood. She mistrusted large areas of grass and woodland. Grass other than corporation grass behind railings was outside her experience and such woodland as she knew in the ordinary way in Luston was no place to take thirteen-year-old twins.

"Let's go in them woods, Mum," suggested Maureen.

"No."

"Why not?"

Mrs. Fisher set her lips. Like Disraeli, she never apologized, she never explained. She took a deep breath. "You'll have your sandwiches over there by them graves."

"I don't want to go near the moldy old church," protested Maureen, but both the twins recognized the note of flat command in their mother's voice and obediently settled themselves down among the headstones. Afterwards, while waiting for the next conducted tour of the house to begin, they went inside the church.

In view of what was to happen later, this was a pity.

True, Mrs. Fisher promptly sat down in a pew and eased off her shoes, but it was too early in what was to prove a very long day for her to have any real benefit from this short period of shoelessness. Besides, there was the discomfort of getting feet back into shoes now too small ...

While she sat there Michael and Maureen scampered about the church in a singularly uninhibited fashion. Mrs. Fisher had noticed before that there had been no wonder left in either twin since they had gone to a brand new comprehensive school in the middle of Luston that had everything—including showers, which Mrs. Fisher didn't think were quite nice. (This last opinion was in no wise influenced by the fact that there were no bathrooms in Paradise Row.)

Not unexpectedly, the chief objects of interest to the Fishers in the little church were connected with the Ornums. The family pew, for instance, with its coat of arms emblazoned on the wooden door. Strictly speaking, both family pew and coat of arms should doubtless have gone with the abolition of pew rents, but as the Earl of Ornum was patron of the living the question had—somehow—never arisen.

"Mum ..." That was Michael.

"What is it now?"

"What does 'atone' mean?"

"What do you want to know for?" temporized Mrs. Fisher.

"It's on this picture thing." Michael traced out the heraldic lettering on the coat of arms with a grubby finger. "It says here, 'I will atone.' "

"Does it?" said Mrs. Fisher with genuine interest. "I wonder what they got up to then?"

But Michael Fisher had by then moved on to a tomb where a stone man lay in effigy, his stone wife by his side, his stone hands clasped round the hilt of a sword. A little stone dog lay at his feet—which Mrs. Fisher thought silly—and his legs were crossed, which privately Mrs. Fisher thought sillier still. Everyone knew you straightened out someone's legs when he died. Mrs. Fisher, who had been in at nearly every death in Paradise Row since she married (marriage was the emotional coming-of-age in her part of Luston), lost interest in that particular Earl of Ornum who had gone to the Crusades.

Maureen was standing before a much later memorial. There was enough color still to attract the eye to this one and a lot of gold lettering on black marble. Two figures—man and wife—were kneeling opposite each other. On either side of them was a row of smaller kneeling figures.

"Four, five, six … six girls," Maureen called across to her mother.

"Don't shout," said Mrs. Fisher automatically.

"Mum, there's six little girls on this grave thing. Aren't they sweet? And four little boys."

"Them's their children," said Mrs. Fisher. "Big families they had then." Mrs. Fisher was one of nine herself. There was something very nice about big families. And as for the children in them—well, her own mother used to say children in big families were born with the corners rubbed off. Which was more than you could say for the twins.

Maureen wasn't listening. "I've found some more children round the side, Mum, only you can't tell whether they're boys or girls …"

Mrs. Fisher got to her feet. "Time we was going," she said decisively.

"What are they round the side like that for, Mum?" Maureen Fisher was nothing if not persistent. "You can hardly see them."

Mrs. Pearl Fisher—without benefit of ecclesiology, so to speak—could guess. The tapestry of life in Paradise Row was every bit as colorful and interwoven as that of the aristocracy—only the middle classes were dull. Aloud she said, "I couldn't say, I'm sure. Now, come along, do …"

They walked across from the church to the house.

Maureen sniffed. "Lilac blossom everywhere," she said with deep contentment.

"Only on the lilac trees," her twin corrected her.

Mrs. Fisher scolded them both with fine impartiality and they joined a small queue of people who were waiting to go inside the house. It was a queue that was turned into a party with one collective sweep of the guide's eyes.

That was Mr. Feathers.

He was a retired schoolmaster who lived in the neighboring village of Petering. There were several guides at Ornum House and their work was done on the principle of one guide per public room rather than one guide per party. This was the fruit of experience. One guide per room ensured the safety of the room and contents. There had been lost—not to say, black—sheep in the days when it had been one guide per party.

"Is that the Earl, Mum?" asked Maureen loudly.

"No," said Mrs. Fisher, though for the life of her she couldn't have said why she was so sure. Perhaps it was because this man had glasses. Earls, she thought, didn't wear glasses.

Mr. Feathers, having assembled his flock, led them into the great hall.

"Early Tudor," he said without preamble, trying to assess the group and measure their interest in such things as king posts and hammer beams. He positioned himself in the center of the floor. "When they first built this room they used to have the fire where I'm standing now ..."

"What about the smoke?" asked someone.

"The smoke," continued Mr. Feathers smoothly, "was left to find its own way out as best it could. As you can see"—here he pointed upwards, past a substantial chandelier, towards the roof—"it ... er ... kippered the beams very nicely."

Thirty-five pairs of eyes obediently looked towards the roof. The thirty-sixth pair belonged to Michael Fisher, who was taking a potentially dangerous interest in the inner workings of a very fine clock by Thomas Tompion. Fortunately the thirty-seventh pair was watching Michael Fisher. Mr. Feathers had forty years' teaching experience behind him and was quite capable of pointing in one direction and looking in another. He also knew the vulnerable places in the great hall and bore down upon Michael at speed.

Michael's mother, who was usually the first person to stop Michael doing something, was perversely annoyed when Mr. Feathers did so.

She was hotly defensive at once.

"He never touched it," she said, though in fact she had been looking at the kippered beams at the time. "Not a finger did that child ..."

Mr. Feathers' voice carried easily and clearly across the great hall and above hers. "After about a hundred years they got tired of choking from the smoke and in 1609 they put in the chimney at the far end."

Everyone—including Michael Fisher this time—looked at the chimney and fireplace. It was a truly magnificent affair, running for half the width of the far end of the room. Inside it was space enough for a dozen people. There was a huge andiron there on which rested several young tree trunks by way of winter fuel. Behind was a fireback carrying the same heraldic message as did that on the family pew.

"What does it mean, Mum?" hissed Maureen, sotto voce.

"Property of the Earl of Ornum," said Mrs. Fisher smartly. "Same as on the corporation buses."

Mr. Feathers cleared his throat and resumed his hortatory address. "The little cupboards on either side of the fire were for salt. That way it was always kept dry. Salt, you know, had quite some significance in olden days. It was by way of being a status symbol—"

"Below the salt," put in a rather earnest-looking woman, who was clutching *A Guide to Calleshire*.

"Exactly."

Mrs. Fisher changed her not inconsiderable weight from one foot to the other and wished she could sit down. The only status symbol recognized in Paradise Row was a wedding ring—which served to remind her of Mavis Palmer and her young man, Bernard. If she was any judge, Mavis would be needing one fairly soon.

Mr. Feathers turned back to the center of the hall and sketched a quick word picture for them. "You can imagine what it must have been like here in the old days. The Earl and his family sat on that dais over there—"

"Above the salt," chimed in the earnest one irritatingly.

"And his servants and retainers below the salt in the main body of the hall. He would have had his own men-at-arms, you know, and one or two of them would always have been on guard." Mr. Feathers gave a pedantic chuckle. "The floor wouldn't have been as clean then as it is just now ..."

Pearl Fisher—Pearl Hipps, that was, before her marriage to Mr. Fisher— was with him at once. As a girl she had seen the film in which Charles Laughton had tossed his chicken leg over his shoulder with a fine abandon. Henry the Eighth, she thought, but Charles Laughton she was sure.

That had been in the days when she sat in the back row of the one and ninepennies at the flicks with Fred Carter. Actually they only paid ninepence and then used to creep backwards when the lights went out, but it came to the same thing. Mrs. Fisher came out of a reverie that included Fred Carter (he had been a lad, all right) and inflation (you couldn't get a cinema seat for ninepence these days) to see Mr. Feathers, his back to the fireplace now, pointing to the opposite end of the room above the dais.

A minstrels' gallery ran across the entire width of the great hall.

"The music came from up there," said Mr. Feathers, "though it was music of a somewhat different variety from that which you would hear today. They would have had lutes, and probably a virginal ..."

"Mum," Maureen Fisher tugged at her mother's sleeve. "Mum, what's a virginal?"

Mrs. Fisher, having no ready answer to this, slapped her daughter instead.

"And," continued Mr. Feathers, "they would have played up there, quite unseen, during the evening meal. Now, look up that way and a little to the left. . . . Do you see up there—in the corner at the back of the minstrels' gallery ..."

"A little window," contributed someone helpfully.

"A little window," agreed Mr. Feathers. "Behind it there is a small room. From there the Earl would keep an eye on what everyone was getting up to." He spoke at large—but he looked at Michael Fisher.

"And they couldn't see him," said a voice in a group.

"No." Mr. Feathers smiled a schoolmaster's smile. "They couldn't see him."

Several necks craned upwards towards the peephole, but it was in shadow—as its Tudor creators had intended it should be. There was no light behind the window and it would be quite impossible to tell if there was anyone looking through it or not.

"For all we know," said Mr. Feathers in a mock-sinister voice, "there may be someone there now, watching us."

What the reaction of his listeners to this suggestion was, Mr. Feathers never knew. At that very moment there was a terrible screech. It rang through the great hall and must have come from somewhere not far away. It was eldritch, hideous.

And utterly inhuman.

It was almost as if the sound had been deliberately laid on as a Maskelyne-type distraction, because when it had died away Mrs. Fisher became aware that Michael had completely disappeared.

2

Whatever else was in short supply in Paradise Row, emotion and drama were never stinted.

"Whatever's that?" gasped Mrs. Fisher, clutching her heart and looking round wildly. "And where's my Michael?" She pointed. "Over there, that's where it came from."

"Outside anyway," said a thin woman in sensible shoes, as if this absolved her from any further action.

"Sounds to me as if someone was being murdered," insisted Mrs. Fisher.

Mr. Feathers shook his head. "Peacocks," he explained briefly. "On the terrace."

Mrs. Fisher was unconvinced. "Peacocks?"

Maureen Fisher had already gone off in the direction of the noise and was starting to climb on a chair the better to see out of the window.

This galvanized Mr. Feathers into near frenzy. "Get down, girl," he shouted. "No one's stood on that chair since Chippendale made it and you're not going to be the first."

Maureen backed down. "I only wanted to see ..."

"Gave me quite a turn, it did," declared Mrs. Fisher generally, looking round the party in a challenging fashion. Wherever she looked there was indubitably no sign of Michael.

The earnest woman—she who carried *The Guide to Calleshire*—and who had hardly done more than start at the noise, smiled distantly, and the whole group began to move towards one of the doors leading off the great hall. Mr. Feathers promised there would be another guide upstairs, made absolutely sure Michael Fisher wasn't hiding anywhere, and then turned back to his next party.

Mrs. Fisher, thinking about her feet and her Michael, shuffled along in the group towards the staircase. In Paradise Row a bare wooden staircase meant you couldn't afford a carpet. In Ornum House it obviously meant something quite different. For one fleeting moment it crossed Mrs. Fisher's mind how wonderful it must have been to have swept down that staircase in a long dress—and then someone trod on her toe and instantly she was back in the present.

And there was still no sign of Michael.

There were pictures lining the staircase wall, small dark oil paintings in the Dutch style, which did not appeal to Mrs. Fisher though she liked the gold frames well enough, but there was a portrait on the landing at the head of the stairs which caught her eye.

Literally.

The sitter must have been looking at the artist because whichever way Mrs. Pearl Fisher looked at the portrait, the portrait looked back at Mrs. Pearl Fisher. It was of a woman, a woman in a deep red velvet dress, against which the pink of a perfect complexion stood out. But it was neither her clothes—which Mrs. Fisher thought of as costume—nor her skin which attracted Mrs. Fisher. It was her face.

It had a very lively look indeed.

And of one thing Mrs. Fisher was quite sure. Oil painting or not, the woman in the portrait had been no better than she ought to have been.

"This way, please," called the next guide. "Now, this is the long gallery ..."

Michael wasn't there.

By comparison with the lady on the landing Mrs. Fisher found the portraits in the long gallery dull.

"Lely, Romney, Gainsborough," chanted Miss Cleepe, a short-sighted maiden lady from Ornum village in charge of the Long Gallery, who recited her litany of fashionable portrait painters at half hourly intervals throughout the season. By June she had lost any animation she might have had in April. "That's the eleventh Earl and Countess on either side of the fireplace in their coronation robes for Edward the Seventh—"

"Who's the one outside?" Mrs. Fisher wanted to know. She jerked her finger over her shoulder. "You know, on the landing."

Miss Cleepe pursed her lips. "That's the Lady Elizabeth Murton. She's dead now. . . . Now, ladies and gentlemen, if you will look back at the coronation paintings you will see a very good representation of the Earl's coronet ..."

"This picture," said Mrs. Fisher.

"The coronet," went on Miss Cleepe gamely, "has eight balls on tall spikes in alternation with eight strawberry leaves ..."

Mrs. Fisher, who did not in any case know what a coronet was, was not interested. "This Lady Elizabeth ..." she persisted.

Miss Cleepe gave in. "Yes?"

"Who was she?"

Miss Cleepe turned back reluctantly, and said very slowly, "She was a daughter of the house."

"What did she do?"

"Do?"

"To be put out there?"

Miss Cleepe looked confused. "She made rather an unfortunate marriage."

"Ohoh," said Mrs. Fisher.

"With her groom."

"They ran away together …" supplied Mrs. Fisher intuitively.

"I believe so."

Somewhere at the back of the party someone said lightly, "Why didn't they just turn the picture to the wall?"

This had the effect of making Miss Cleepe more confused than ever. "Her son, Mr. William Murton, still comes here."

Mrs. Fisher gave a satisfied nod. "That's why she's on the landing."

"Yes." Miss Cleepe paused, and then—surprisingly—ventured a piece of information quite outside her usual brief. "She was known locally, I understand, as Bad Betty."

Mrs. Fisher looked around the rest of the party and said cheerfully, "They're no different here really, are they? Same as my cousin Alfred. No one's got any photographs of him any more. Or if they have, they don't put them in the front parlor."

"The most valuable painting in the long gallery," Miss Cleepe hastened to reassert herself, "is that one over there. In the middle of the right-hand wall."

Everyone stared at a rather dark oil.

"It's by Holbein. Painted in 1532. It's of a member of the family who went in for law. Judge Cremond."

The subject of the picture was fingering a small black cap.

"It's popularly known as The Black Death," said Miss Cleepe.

The group looked suitably impressed. The only exception was an artistic-looking young man with long hair who held that the female form was the only subject worth painting.

Miss Cleepe paused for dramatic effect. "And it's his ghost who still haunts the great hall …"

"I thought you'd have a ghost," said someone with satisfaction.

Miss Cleepe nodded. She was absolutely sure of her audience now. "He was a judge and he sentenced the wrong man to death. His soul can't rest, you see …"

The sightseeing party was almost equally divided into those who believed every word and the skeptics who believed nothing.

"That," said Miss Cleepe, "is where the family motto comes from."

" 'I will atone,' " said Mrs. Fisher promptly. She was, of course, numbered among the believers, her mother having hand-reared her on fable rather than fact.

"He doesn't look the sort of man to let something like that put him out," observed a man in the party. A skeptic.

This was true. The thin lips which stretched across under the unmistakably Cremond nose, a nose common to all the family portraits, did not look as if their owner would have been unduly disturbed by the odd death or two in what were admittedly stirring times.

"Ah," said Miss Cleepe melodramatically, "but it was his own son who died. And now, whenever a member of the family is about to die, the Judge walks abroad."

The skeptics continued to look skeptical and the believers believing.

"And next to that is a portrait of the ninth Earl as a young man. That's a falcon on his wrist ..." Miss Cleepe suddenly dived away from the party, showing a surprising fleetness of foot. She reached a priceless orrery just as Maureen Fisher was starting it spinning round.

"We got one at school anyway," she said, "and it's better than this."

"No, you haven't," retorted Miss Cleepe crisply. "This is an orrery. What you have is a globe. That shows you the world. This is about space."

Maureen Fisher looked skeptically at the antique inlaid wood. "Space?"

"Space," said Miss Cleepe. She raised her voice in the manner of all guides to include the whole party, and went on, "In the olden days the ladies of the house would spend much of their time in this room. When it was wet they would take their exercise in here." She pointed out of the far window. "On fine days they would walk in the park—perhaps to the folly."

They all stared across towards the distant folly. There was no sign whatever of Miss Mavis Palmer and her young man, Bernard. Mrs. Fisher wished Miss Cleepe hadn't mentioned walking. For a few precious minutes—while thinking about the errant Lady Elizabeth Murton—she had managed to forget both her feet and the fact that Michael was still missing. Now they came into the forefront of her mind again.

"Who is the man in armor?" asked the earnest woman, indicating a painting near the far door. "It looks like a Rembrandt."

"No." Miss Cleepe shook her head. "It's quite modern, though it doesn't look it. The twelfth Earl—that is the father of the present Earl—was a great collector of medieval armor. You'll see the armory presently, those of you who want to go down there."

"Yes," said Maureen Fisher simply.

"The Earl had himself painted in a suit of armor which used to belong to one of his ancestors."

They all peered curiously at the painting of the helmeted figure.

"Sort of fancy dress?" said Mrs. Fisher dubiously.

"You could say that," said Miss Cleepe. "Now, if you'll all go through that door there and then round to the right ..."

Mrs. Fisher shuffled along with the crowd, uneasily aware that Maureen was getting bored and—which was worse—that Michael still wasn't anywhere to be seen.

"Perhaps," suggested Maureen cheerfully, "the ghost's got him."

The next room was the solarium.

"The what?" asked Mrs. Fisher of the woman beside her.

"Solarium," said the woman.

"What's that?"

The next guide explained, and then passed them along to the main bedroom. The lady in charge of the bedroom was a Mrs. Nutting.

("Job for a married woman, that," his Lordship had declared. "No use putting Miss Cleepe there."

Charles Purvis had agreed and had found Mrs. Nutting.)

Mrs. Nutting was well aware of the main points of interest in the bedroom.

No, the present Earl and Countess did not sleep in the fourposter.

Yes, fourposters were rather short.

And high.

The ceiling was very beautiful.

Yes, it was like lacework.

Or icing.

The bobble was the Tudor Rose.

It was called pargetting.

Maureen Fisher tugged at her mother's sleeve. "Them curtains round the bed, Mum, what are they for?"

"Warmth," replied Mrs. Fisher tersely, her eyes for once on the guide.

For Mrs. Nutting had moved across to a corner of the bedroom towards a great mahogany cupboard. More than half of the party expected a wardrobe full of robes—ermine at least. What was inside the cupboard was a miniature bathroom.

"The twelfth Earl had it put there," said Mrs. Nutting. "Of course, you can't lie down in the bath, but it was as good as the old-fashioned hip bath of the day. You see the wash-hand basin first and then round to the right—the bath itself."

Mrs. Fisher was enchanted.

She wasn't one of those who was ambling through the rooms of the house in a pipe dream of vicarious ownership. She didn't see her own home as a minuscule of what she saw in Ornum House. She didn't even have any reproduction furniture on whose quality she could now congratulate herself.

Nor was she seeking to reassure herself that the gap between the Fishers of this world and the Ornums was small—she knew it wasn't. And two minutes ago she would have sworn she wasn't going to go back to Paradise Row and change anything.

But a bathroom in a cupboard.

There was room for a cupboard in Paradise Row but not a bathroom. She moved closer.

"Before then," expanded Mrs. Nutting, "hot water was brought up here in great copper jugs, but the twelfth Earl designed this himself and had it fitted here. It hardly takes up any room at all …"

That was true.

The party, sheeplike, started to follow their leader towards the bedroom door. Mrs. Fisher was the last to leave. She was studying the miniature bath.

There was still no sign of Michael. She hardly took in any of the drawing room for thinking about him.

"Originally the withdrawing room," explained Mrs. Mompson, the over-refined widow of a former doctor of Ornum who was graciously pleased—as she herself put it—to "help out the Earl with the visitors."

"Not, of course," she added, "a room in which actual drawing was done."

Mrs. Fisher did not listen. Gnawing anxiety about Michael had succeeded mild concern. Whereabouts in this vast house was he, and, more important, what was he up to?

After the drawing room came another room, smaller but made infinitely charming by a most beautiful collection of china and porcelain. It lined the walls in cleverly illuminated glass cases. Momentarily—only momentarily—Mrs. Fisher was glad that Michael was out of the way of harming it.

Those members of the public who had come—whether they admitted it or not—hoping for a glimpse of "the family" never knew—never even suspected—the woman in charge of the china.

"Very early Wedgwood mostly," said Miss Gertrude Cremond, cousin to the present Earl. She had a gruff voice which carried well and, in spite of the heat, wore an old cardigan. "Some Meissen and Sèvres brought back by the family from the Continent on their travels. Grand Tours and so forth …"

This was her private joke.

"And a little Ming bought in when they could afford it."

This was her public joke.

She was a vigorous woman of indeterminate age. She had played hockey for Calleshire in her youth and still looked as if a distant cry of "sticks" would distract her from the business in hand. She had never married and now her home was with her cousin, the Earl. She looked after the china and did the flowers and the myriad of other small inconsequential tasks that were at one and the same time above and beyond the housekeeper but too mundane for the Countess.

She did all the china herself and very occasionally in the crowd found a kindred spirit.

Not today.

"Lovely, isn't it?"

"We have a little Wedgwood bowl at home."

"Glad I don't have to clean it all."

"I do," responded Miss Cremond, thus dispelling any suspicions in anyone's mind that she could possibly be other than hired help.

There were clucks of sympathy all round at the enormity of the task, but soon they shuffled on. Like all such visitors they came, they saw, they fingered, they exclaimed, they went.

It was almost exactly an hour after leaving it that the party arrived back in the great hall.

The discomfort from her feet was vying in Mrs. Fisher's mind with the constant fret about Michael—and with the interest of the bathroom. What she wanted more than anything else was a chair that didn't have a red cord stretched from arm to arm. It seemed, though, that the tour was not yet at an end. Mr. Feathers was speaking to them again.

"Those of you who wish may now go down to the dungeons and armory at no extra charge." He paused. "The twelfth Earl assembled one of the finest collections of medieval armor in the country. However, I must warn you that the stair is difficult."

This last would have settled it for Mrs. Fisher and her poor feet had Michael not been missing. Mr. Feathers had not seen him. He was quite certain about this, declaring that he would know Michael anywhere.

"Like Maureen but a boy," said Mrs. Fisher by way of describing him.

Mr. Feathers said with perfect truth that he remembered Michael only too well and he was sure he hadn't seen him since Mrs. Fisher's party had left the great hall.

"The armory," he suggested. "Perhaps he went down there."

Mr. Feathers had been right to winnow out the party. This was no staircase for the aged and infirm. It was not wood but stone and it wound its way down inside a turret. A hanging rope did duty as a banister, but Mrs. Fisher did not trust it. Instead she pressed herself against the outer wall, invisibly helped by a force she did not recognize as centrifugal.

"We know one thing about the chap who built this," called out Mr. Feathers cheerfully from above. "He was left-handed. This staircase goes round the wrong way. That was so that his sword arm would be free."

Mrs. Fisher did not care.

The descending stair seemed interminable. She had no idea how many times it wound round. She concentrated on following the person ahead and trying to keep out of the way of the person behind. At long last the steps came to an end and she was on a level floor again. It was very gloomy.

"I don't like it down here, Mum," complained Maureen. "It's too dark."

This was true: the only lighting came from two low-powered sconces on the wall.

("Don't overdo the electricity down there, Purvis."

"Very well, my lord."

"Got to get the right atmosphere.")

As far as Mrs. Fisher was concerned they'd got it. She shivered and wished she was somewhere else. Just wait until she found Michael, that's all, she wouldn't half give him …

"This way for the dungeons." That was Bert Hackle, one of the undergardeners at Ornum House. He was custodian of the dungeons and tackled the job with relish. "This way, please."

His voice boomed back from the bare stone walls and his boots grated on the floor much as those of a jailer would have done. Mrs. Fisher shivered again.

"This is the oldest part of the house," he announced. "Left over from when it was a castle. All the rest was built on top of this bit and lots more that's gone through the centuries."

He waited for the echo to catch up with him.

"This bit here," he put his hand on a stone wall that could only be called substantial, "is what used to be a bastion."

"Well I never," murmured someone obligingly.

"And inside it is the donjon, or dungeon," said Bert Hackle, giving Mrs. Fisher her first and last lesson in philology. "Donjon—dungeon. See?"

He led the way round the wall, and stooping, went through an arch where a door had been. They crowded in after him. "This is where they kept the prisoners."

His party was suitably impressed.

"Nasty, isn't it?"

"Glad I wasn't one."

"Look at that damp. If they didn't have anything else they'd soon have rheumatism."

This last was an unfair reflection on the original builders, whose stone-work had, in fact, been perfect. The dampness could be laid entirely at Bert Hackle's door. The instinct of an undergardener is to sprinkle water everywhere and Bert Hackle had lent a touch of verisimilitude to the dungeon walls by the judicious application of a little water before visit-ing time.

His Lordship—who was not slow—had done nothing to stop him. In-deed, on the last occasion he had been down there, the Earl had gone so far as to congratulate Bert on the fern species which were growing from a crack in the wall.

("Fine plant you have there, Hackle," he had said.

"Thank you, my lord.")

Which Bert had taken as tacit approval.

"There'll be a well somewhere," said someone in the party who knew about castles.

Bert Hackle pointed. "Over there."

The castle well was deep enough to need no faking and had been firmly boarded over on the advice of his Lordship's insurance company.

"Good water," said the gardener. "Nice and sweet."

"Better than the piped stuff," said a woman who had heard of—but knew nothing about—typhoid fever.

Hackle moved beyond the well head and took up a fresh stance in front of a low grating cut in the side of the wall. He cleared his throat impres-sively. The echo didn't quite know what to make of this and there was an appreciable pause before he began on what was obviously his *pièce de résistance*.

"If you was bad," he said, "you were thrown into the dungeons, but if you was really bad ..."

Mrs. Fisher was sure Michael must be about somewhere.

"If you was really bad, they put you in here." He bent his powerful arms down and pulled at the two iron bars of the grating. A great stone pivoted outwards, revealing a hole beyond. Three men might have stood in it.

"It's a n'oobliette," announced Hackle. "Where you put your prisoners and forgot them."

"From the French," translated the earnest woman.

Mrs. Fisher craned her neck to make sure that Michael wasn't in it.

"They had it just here," Hackle said in a macabre voice, "so that the prisoners could see the water being brought up from the well. Then they didn't give them none."

It took everyone except Mrs. Fisher a little time to sort out this double negative.

"They died of thirst," she said at once, "while they was watching the water."

Bert Hackle sucked his lips. "That's right. Now, if you'll all come along here with me I'll show you the way to the armory. It's been reconstitooted from part of the old curtain wall …"

But the *oubliette*—or perhaps the stone staircase—had been enough for some, and the party that eventually entered the armory was a very thin one. The earnest woman came—of course—and some three or four others.

"Michael Fisher!" Michael Fisher's mother gave a shriek of mingled anger and recognition. "You naughty boy! You wait until I get you home …"

"It's lovely down here, Mum."

"What ever do you mean by running away like that?"

"It's much more fun down here." Michael remained undismayed by her anger.

Mrs. Fisher took a quick look round. There was one thing about this part of the house that reassured her. The old things, having stood the test of so very much time, were more likely to stand the test of Michael Fisher. His mother did not think he could have got up to much in the armory.

Wherein she was sadly wrong.

It was a truly fearsome collection. Weapons sprouted from the walls, antique swords lay about in glass cases, chain-mail hung from hooks, and—as if this weren't enough—several suits of armor stood about on the floor.

"Whoopee," shouted Michael. "Look, Mum, this is what I've been doing."

He darted off down the center of the armory, shadowboxing with the coat of war of some long-forgotten knight of a bygone age.

"Got you," he said to one of them, landing a blow on the breastplate. It resounded across the hall.

"Mum …" This was Maureen, who had been studying the contents of one of the glass cases without real interest.

"What?"

"Mum, what's a belt of chastity?"

Mrs. Fisher's answer to this was what the psychologists call a displacement activity. She shouted at her son.

"Michael, leave that suit of armor alone."

"I just want to look inside."

"Leave it alone, I tell you."

The earnest woman looked up at the raised voice and politely looked away again.

Michael was struggling with the visor.

"Can't you hear what I say?"

There was at least no doubt about that. Mrs. Fisher in full voice could be heard clearly from one end of Paradise Row to the other, so the armory presented no problem in audibility.

"Yes, I just want to …" Michael heaved at the visor with both hands.

"Mum …" It was a whine from Maureen. "Mum, what's a belt of chastity?"

"Michael Fisher, you'll leave that suit of armor alone or else …"

What the alternative was no one ever knew. At that moment Michael Fisher managed to lift the visor.

He stared inside.

A face stared back at him.

It was human and it was dead.

3

The information was not exactly welcomed at the nearest police station. In fact, the Superintendent of Police in Berebury was inclined to be petulant when he was told. He glared across his desk at the head of his Criminal Investigation Department and said:

"You sure it isn't a false alarm, malicious intent?"

"A body in a suit of armor," repeated Detective Inspector C.D. Sloan, the bearer of the unhappy news.

"Perhaps it was a dummy," said Superintendent Leeyes hopefully. "False alarm, good intent."

"In Ornum House," went on Sloan.

"Ornum House?" The superintendent sat up. He didn't like the sound of that at all. "You mean the place where they have all those day trippers?"

"Yes, sir." Sloan didn't suppose the people who paid their half crowns to go round Ornum House thought of themselves as day trippers, but there was no good going into that with the superintendent now.

"Whereabouts in Ornum House is this body?"

Sloan coughed. "In the armory, actually, sir."

"I might have known," grunted Leeyes. "In that sort of setup the armor is always in the armory."

"Yes, sir."

"Who said so?"

Sloan started. "The steward."

"Not"—heavily sarcastic—"not the butler?"

"No, sir. He's gone down to keep guard. The steward—his name's Purvis—came to telephone us."

"And," asked Leeyes pertinently, "the name of the body in the armor?"

"He didn't say, sir. He just said his Lordship was sure we would wish to know."

The superintendent glared suspiciously at his subordinate. "He did, did he?"

"Yes, sir."

Leeyes took a deep breath. "Then you'd better go and—what is it they say?—unravel the mystery, hadn't you, Sloan?"

"Yes, sir."

"Though I don't want any touching of forelocks, kowtowing or what have you, Sloan. This is the twentieth century."

"Yes, sir."

"On the other hand"—very silkily—"you would do well to remember that the Earl of Ornum is a Deputy Lieutenant for Calleshire."

"I shan't forget, sir." Even though it was the twentieth century?

"Now, who have you got to go with you?"

"Only Detective Constable Crosby"—apologetically.

Leeyes groaned. "Crosby?"

"Sergeant Gelven's gone on that training course, if you remember, sir."

The Criminal Investigation Department at Berebury was a very small affair, all matters of great criminal moment being referred to the County Constabulary Headquarters at Calleford.

The superintendent snorted gently. "I shouldn't have thought Crosby could unravel knitting let alone some masochistic nonsense like this."

"No, sir." But it would have to be Crosby because there wasn't anyone else.

"All right," sighed Leeyes. "Take him—but do try to see that he doesn't say 'You can't do that there 'ere' to the Earl."

Detective Constable Crosby—raw, but ambitious, too—drove Inspector Sloan the odd fifteen miles or so from the police station at Berebury to the village of Ornum. The village itself was clustered about the entrance to the park—and it was a very imposing entrance indeed. Crosby turned the car in between two magnificent wrought-iron gates.

The gates were painted black, with the finer points etched out in gold leaf. If the state of a man's gate was any guide to the man—and in Sloan's working experience it was—the Earl of Ornum maintained a high standard. Surmounting the pillars were two stone spheres, and crouching on top of the spheres was a pair of gryphons.

Constable Crosby regarded them critically. "They're funny-looking birds, aren't they? Can't say I've ever seen anything like that flying around."

"I'm glad to hear it, Constable. They don't exist."

Crosby glanced up over his shoulder at the solid stone. "I see, sir."

"A myth," amplified Sloan. "Like unicorns."

"Yes, sir." Crosby slid the car between the gryphons and lowered his speed to a self-conscious fifteen miles an hour in deference to a notice which said just that. Then he cleared his throat. "The house, sir. I can't see it."

"Stately homes aren't meant to be seen from the road, Constable. That's the whole idea. Carry on."

Crosby subsided into silence—for perhaps half a minute. "It's a long way, sir ..."

Sloan grunted. "The distance in this instance between the rich man in his castle and the poor man at his gate is about a mile."

"A mile, sir?" Crosby digested this, dropping a gear the while. This particular police car wasn't used to a steady fifteen m.p.h.

"A mile," confirmed Sloan, whose own single latched gate led up a short straight path to a semidetached house in suburban Berebury. In his view his own path had the edge—so to speak—on the Earl's inasmuch as it was flanked by prize rose bushes as opposed to great oak trees. Sloan favored roses. He felt that there should be a moratorium on crime while they were in bloom.

"Sir, if we were to go over fifteen miles an hour would a prosecution hold under the Road Traffic Acts?" Crosby was young still and anxious for promotion. "They'd have to bring a private prosecution, wouldn't they? I mean, we couldn't bring one, or could we?"

Sloan, who was watching keenly for a first glimpse of Ornum House, said, "Couldn't do what?"

"Bring a prosecution for speeding on private land." Crosby kept his eye on the speedometer. "Traffic Division wouldn't be able to do a thing, would they?"

Sloan grunted. Traffic Division were never ones for being interested in the finer academic points of law. Their line of demarcation was a simple one.

Fatals and non-fatals.

However, if Crosby wanted to split hairs ...

"Going over the limit anytime, anywhere, Constable, isn't the same thing as proving it."

"No, sir, but if you had two independent witnesses ..."

"Ah," said Sloan drily. "I agree that would be different." He peered forward, thinking he saw a building. "I don't know when I last saw two independent witnesses. Rare birds, independent witnesses. I'd put them in the same category as gryphons myself."

Crosby persisted, "But if you had them, sir, then what? I could ask Traffic, I suppose ..."

Sloan happened to know that Inspector Harpe of Traffic Division wouldn't thank anybody for asking him anything else just at this moment. Superintendent Leeyes had today posed him about the most awkward question a police officer could ever be asked. It was: "Why were all the damaged cars from the accident jobs attended by his three crews finding their way into the same garage for repair? If anyone was getting a rake-off there would be hell to pay ..."

"Sir," Crosby pointed suddenly. "Something moved over there between the trees. I saw it."

Sloan turned and caught a glimpse of brown. "Deer. And there's the house coming up now. Keep going."

There was a young woman sitting by a baize-covered table near the front door. She had on a pretty summer frock and she was all for charging Sloan and Crosby half a crown before she would let them in.

"Half a crown, did you say, miss?" Sloan was torn between a natural reluctance to tell anyone who didn't already know that the police had been sent for—and the certain knowledge of the difficulty he would have in retrieving five shillings from the County Council No. 2 Imprest Account, police officers, for the use of.

"Half a crown if you want to go into the house," she said firmly. "Gardens and the park only, a shilling."

They were rescued—just in time—by a competent-looking young man who introduced himself as Charles Purvis, steward and comptroller to the Earl of Ornum.

"That's all right, Lady Eleanor," he said. "These two gentlemen have come to see me. They're not visitors."

She nodded and turned to give change to the next arrivals.

The steward led the two policemen through the great hall—Mr. Feathers was saying his piece there to a fresh party—and then down the spiral staircase.

"We closed the armory at once, Inspector—you'll watch your step here, won't you ..."

Sloan was going to watch his step in Ornum House all right. He had his pension to think of.

"Shall I go first, Inspector?" offered Purvis. "It's a bit tricky on the downward flight."

It wasn't only going to be the staircase that was tricky either. Sloan could see that already.

"Hang on to the rope," advised Charles Purvis. "As I was saying, we closed the armory at once but didn't tell more people than was absolutely necessary."

"Not Lady Eleanor?" said Sloan.

"No, she doesn't know yet." Purvis turned left at the bottom of the staircase and led the way down the dim corridor. "We felt it would only cause comment to close the entire house at this stage."

A body in the armory of a stately home was going to do more than cause comment, but Sloan did not say so. Instead, he murmured something about not letting those with were in the house out.

"The earlier parties will have gone by now," said Purvis regretfully. "The armory is the last of the rooms on exhibition because relatively few people are interested. They mostly don't come down here at all, but go into the park next."

They passed the dungeon and the well head and found Bert Hackle standing guard at the armory door.

"There's nobody here now, Mr. Purvis, but me. Mr. Dillow—"

"The butler," put in Purvis.

"That's right," said Bert Hackle. "He's taken all those that were in here along to the kitchen with Mrs. Morley."

"Thank you, Hackle." Purvis opened the armory door and walked in, the two policemen at his heels.

At first glance it did not seem as if anything was amiss.

All was still and the room resembled a museum gallery as much as anything. There were eight suits of armor, each standing attentively facing the center of the room as if alert for some fresh call to arms. Sloan regarded them closely. The visors were down on all of them, but one at least was more than a mere shell.

"Which …" he began.

"The second on the right," said Charles Purvis.

Sloan and Crosby advanced. A little plaque on the floor in front of it read ARMOR WITH TILT PIECES, CIRCA 1595.

Sloan lifted the visor very very carefully. There might be more fingerprints than those of Michael Fisher here. The visor was heavier than he expected but, just as the boy had done, he got it up at last.

Inside was the face of a man verging on the elderly and more than a little dead. Inspector Sloan touched his cheek though he knew there was no need. It was quite cold. He looked back at the steward.

"Do you know who …"

"Mr. Meredith," supplied Charles Purvis, adding by way of explanation. "Our Mr. Meredith."

"Our Mr. Meredith?"

"Librarian and archivist to his Lordship."

"You know him well then?"

"Oh yes," said the steward readily. "He comes— came—to the house most days. He was writing a history of the family."

"Was he?" Sloan tucked the fact away in his mind. "Where did he live? Here?"

"No. In Ornum village. With his sister."

Sloan lowered the visor. It was just like banishing an unpleasant fact to the back of one's mind. At once the room seemed normal again.

Crosby got out a notebook.

"Mr. Osborne Meredith," said Purvis, "and his address was The Old Forge, Ornum."

"If he came here every day," said Sloan, "perhaps you could tell me the last day you saw him here."

The steward frowned slightly. "Not today, I know."

Sloan knew that too. That cheek had been too chill to the touch.

"I don't recall seeing him yesterday either, now I come to think of it," went on Purvis, "but he might well have been here without my seeing him. He came and went very much as he wished."

Sloan waved a hand in a gesture that took in the whole house. "Whereabouts in here would you expect to see him?"

"He spent most of his time in the library and in the muniments room."

"Did he?" said Sloan, adding ambiguously, "I'll be checking up on that later."

Purvis nodded. "But how he came to be down here in the armory, and in this, Inspector, I couldn't begin to say at all."

"And dead," added Sloan.

"And dead," agreed Purvis somberly. "His Lordship was most distressed when he was told and said that I was to give you every possible assistance …"

"He came and went," observed the egregious Detective Constable Crosby, "and now he's gone."

If anything, Dr. Dabbe, the consultant pathologist to the Berebury group of hospitals, was more put out by the news than the superintendent had been.

But for a different reason. Because it was Sunday afternoon and he was sailing his Albacore at Kinnisport.

"Send him along to the mortuary, Sloan," he said from the yacht club telephone, "and I'll take a look at him when I get back."

The tide must be just right, thought Sloan. Aloud he said, "It's not quite like that, Doctor. The body's at Ornum House."

The medical voice sounded amused. "What are you expecting, Sloan? True blue blood? Because I can assure you that—"

"No, Doctor. It's not like that at all." The telephone that the steward had led him to was in a hallway and rather less private than a public kiosk. "We're treating it as a sudden death."

The sands of time having run out for one more soul.

"Well, then …" said the doctor reasonably.

"He's in a suit of armor for the tilt, circa 1595," said Sloan, "and I not only don't know that we ought to move him, but I'm not at all sure that we can."

Then, duty bound, Sloan telephoned Superintendent Leeyes at Berebury.

"I've been wondering what kept you," said that official pleasantly. "And how did you find the man in the iron mask?"

"Dead," said Sloan.

"Ah!"

"Dead these last couple of days, I should say—though there's not a lot of him visible to go by, if you take my meaning, sir."

Leeyes grunted. "I should have said a good look at the face should have been enough for any really experienced police officer, Sloan."

"Yes, sir." If the deceased had happened to have been shot between the eyes, for instance.

"So?"

"I've sent for Dr. Dabbe, sir, and I'd be obliged if I might have a couple of photographers and a fingerprint man—"

"The lot?"

"Yes, please, sir. And if they'll ask Lady Eleanor to tell the steward when they arrive—"

"Lady who?"

"Lady Eleanor, sir. His Lordship's daughter. She's on duty at the door."

"Is she? Then she'll probably send them round the back anyway," said the superintendent, "when she's taken a good look at them."

"Yes, sir"—dutifully. Then, "The deceased is a Mr. Osborne Meredith, librarian to the Earl."

"Ha!" Triumphantly. "What did I tell you, Sloan? Librarian. He got the idea from a book, I'll be bound. Mark my words, he'll be one of these suicides that's got to be different—"

"Different," conceded Sloan, at once. "This is different all right, but as to the other, sir, I couldn't say. Not yet."

4

Detective Constable Crosby was still keeping watch in the armory when Charles Purvis and Inspector Sloan got back there.

"I've just checked up on the other seven suits of armor, sir," he said virtuously.

"Good."

"All empty."

"Good," said Sloan again, slightly startled this time. Honest as always, even with himself, Sloan admitted that this was something he wouldn't have considered. He'd got a real eager beaver on his hands in young Crosby. Surely Grand Guignol himself wouldn't have thought of seven more men in seven more suits.

"And," went on Crosby, "on the ways into here."

"There's just the one, isn't there?" said Sloan.

"That's right, sir. The door."

Purvis, the steward, seemed inclined to apologize for this. "That's because we're below ground level here, Inspector, and so we can't very well have windows. Nor even borrowed light. It's all artificial, the lighting down here."

Sloan looked round. In a fine imitation of medieval times, flaming-torch-style lighting had been fixed into basket-type brackets high up on the walls.

"The lighting's not very good," said Purvis.

"Effective, though."

Purvis nodded. "Most people are glad to get back upstairs again."

Sloan went back to the second suit of armor on the right. "Tell me, had anyone mentioned to you that Mr. Meredith was missing?"

"No, Inspector. We—that is, I—had no idea at all that everything was not as usual. We shouldn't have opened the house at all today had there been any suggestion that ..." His voice trailed away.

"Quite so," said Sloan.

"Complete surprise to us all." He ran his hand through his hair. "Nasty shock, actually."

"You said he lived with his sister."

"That's right. His Lordship has gone down to Ornum to break the news."

"Himself?"

Purvis looked surprised and a bit embarrassed. "Not the sort of job to delegate, you know. Come better from him anyway, don't you think? Take it as a gesture, perhaps."

"Perhaps."

"Then get the vicar to go round afterwards. Helpful sort of chap, the vicar."

"Good," said Sloan, content that the ground was also being prepared for him. A visit from a humble policeman shouldn't come amiss after all that.

"Though, as to the rest"—the steward waved a hand to embrace the armor—"I can't understand it at all. It's not as if it was even his subject. It's Mr. Ames who's the expert."

"Ames?"

"The vicar. Bit of an enthusiast about armor. If we get any visitors who're really keen we ring him up at the vicarage and he comes in."

Sloan looked round the armory. "There's never a full-time guide here, then?"

"No. Hackle brings people as far as the door when he's finished showing the dungeons and so forth—you need a man there because of the *oubliette*—and then they find their own way out in their own time."

"I see."

Purvis pointed to an arquebus hanging on the wall. "Not everyone's subject."

"No."

"But Mr. Ames catalogued this collection years ago, and he always comes in if special parties come."

"Special parties?"

Purvis nodded. "As well as the ordinary visitors we have what you might call specialist groups. People who are interested in just one facet of Ornum House. Parties come to see the armor and I tell Mr. Ames. It's the same with the pictures and books and manuscript records. Take next week, for instance. I've got a party who call themselves The Young Masters coming down to see the pictures on Monday. Arranged it with Mr. Meredith so that he could ..." Purvis came to a stop when he saw where his sentence was getting him. "Oh, dear, I'd forgotten all about that."

Sloan looked at the suit of armor that contained the late Mr. Meredith and said, "What other ... er ... specialty of the house do you have?"

"The Ornum collection of china," replied the steward, not without pride, "is thought to be one of the finest still in private hands."

"I see." Sloan scratched his chin. "Before I see his Lordship, do you think you could just give me some idea of the setup here?"

"Setup?" said Purvis distantly.

"Who all live here, then ..."

"Well, there's the family, of course ..."

Constable Crosby got out his notebook and started writing.

"There's his Lordship," said Purvis, "and the Countess and their children."

"Lady Eleanor?" said Sloan.

"Lady Eleanor is their only daughter," said Charles Purvis, a curious strangled note creeping into his voice.

"And who else?"

"Lord Cremond, his Lordship's son."

"And heir?" enquired Sloan.

Purvis nodded. "His only son."

"I see. That all?"

The steward smiled faintly. "By no means."

"Oh?"

"Then there's his Lordship's cousin, Miss Gertrude Cremond."

"Quite a family."

"And," went on Purvis, "his Lordship's aunts, Lady Alice and Lady Maude. They are, of course, rather ... er ... elderly now."

Sloan sighed. That, being translated, meant eccentric.

Purvis hadn't finished. "His Lordship's nephew, Mr. Miles Cremond, is staying in the house just now, with his wife, Mrs. Laura Cremond, and then, of course, there are the indoor staff ... Dillow, the butler, and so on."

Sloan sighed again

"Do you want me to go on?" asked Purvis.

"Oh yes," said Sloan grimly, pointing to the suit of armor. "No man could have got into this contraption on his own. I can work that much out from here."

"I know," said Purvis flatly. "That's why we sent for you."

Mrs. Pearl Fisher was sitting in the biggest kitchen Sloan had ever seen in his life.

She was by no means the only person in the room, but she contrived—by a subtle alchemy that would have done credit to some first lady of the stage—to give the impression that she was.

She was sitting at a vast deal table and she was drinking tea. Teas (2/- per head) were available to visitors in the Old stables, but this pot was obviously on the house. It was being administered by the housekeeper, Mrs. Morley, a lady who looked as if she had only just stopped wearing bombazine. A personage whom Sloan took to be Mr. Dillow, the butler, hovered at an appropriate distance.

"I don't know that I'll ever get over the shock," Mrs. Fisher was announcing as Inspector Sloan and Crosby went in.

"The tea will help," Mrs. Morley said drily.

Mrs. Fisher ignored this. "Sent me heart all pitter patter, it did."

"Dear, dear," said Mrs. Morley.

Histrionically, Mrs. Fisher laid her hand on her left chest. "It's still galloping away."

"Another cup of tea?" suggested Mrs. Morley.

Both ladies knew that there would be brandy and to spare in a house like this, but one of them, at least, was not prepared for it to be dispensed.

"It can bring on a nasty turn, can a sight like that," offered Mrs. Fisher.

Mrs. Morley advised a quiet sit.

Mrs. Fisher said she thought it would be quite a while before her heart steadied down again.

Mrs. Morley said she wasn't to think of hurrying. She was very welcome. Besides, the police inspector would want to hear all about it, wouldn't he, sir?

Sloan nodded. Crosby got out his notebook.

"I shall never sleep again," declared Mrs. Fisher. "That face; I tell you, it'll come between me and my sleep for the rest of my born days."

"Tell me, madam—"

"Them eyes," she moaned. "Staring like that."

"Quite so. Now—"

"He didn't die today, did he?" she said. "I know that much—"

"How do you know that?"—sharply.

"He was the same colour as poor old Mr. Wilkins in our street, that's why—"

"Mr. Wilkins?"

"Putty, that's what he looked like when they found him."

"Indeed?"

"Three days' milk there was outside his house before they broke the door down," said Mrs. Fisher reminiscently. "And he looked just like him."

"I see."

"In fact," said Mrs. Fisher, seeing an advantage and taking it all in the same breath, "if it hadn't been for my Michael there's no knowing when you might have found the poor gentleman, is there?" She looked round her audience in a challenging manner. "It's not as if there was any milk bottles."

Sloan nodded. It was a good point. There had been no milk bottles outside the armory door. Nothing that he knew of to lead to that particular suit of armor. There was indeed no knowing …

Where was Michael now?

Michael Fisher, it presently transpired, was somewhere else being sick.

"I don't know what he'll be like in the coach going home, I'm sure," said Mrs. Fisher with satisfaction. "I shouldn't wonder if we don't have to stop."

Maureen was despatched to retrieve Michael.

Finding the dead face had had its effect on the boy. His complexion was chalky white still, and there was a thin line of perspiration along the edge of his hair line. He looked Sloan up and down warily.

"I didn't touch him, mister. I just lifted that front piece thing, that's all."

"Why?" asked Sloan mildly.

"I wanted to see inside."

"But why that particular one? There are eight there."

"Tell the inspector," intruded Mrs. Fisher unnecessarily.

"I dunno why that one."

"Had you touched any of the others?"

Michael licked his lips. "I sort of touched them all."

"Sort of?"

"I'm learning to box at school."

"I see."

"I tried to get under their guards."

"Not too difficult surely?"

"More difficult than you'd think." Michael Fisher's spirit was coming back. "Those arms got in the way."

"But you got round them in the end?"

"That's right."

"And this particular one—the one with the man inside …"

"It sounded different when I hit it," admitted Michael. "Less hollow."

"That's why you looked?"

"Yes."

"No other reason?"

Michael shook his head.

It was the first time in Sloan's police career that he had ever been conducted anywhere by a butler.

"Mr. Purvis said I was to take you straight to his Lordship," said Dillow, "as soon as his Lordship got back from the village."

"Thank you," murmured Sloan politely.

There was no denying that the butler was a man of considerable presence. As tall as the two policemen and graver. Sloan, who had subconsciously expected him to be old, saw that he was no more than middle-aged.

"If you would be so good as to follow me, gentlemen."

Sloan and Crosby obediently fell in behind Dillow of the stately mien and set off on the long journey from the kitchen to what the butler referred to as the private apartments.

"You would have known Mr. Meredith, of course," began Sloan as they rounded their first corridor.

"Certainly, sir. A very quiet gentleman. Always very pleasant, he was. And no trouble."

"Really?" responded Sloan as noncommittally as he could. Mr. Osborne Meredith might not have been any trouble to a butler. He was going to be a great deal of trouble to a police inspector.

This police inspector.

"He usually went home to luncheon," said the butler. "Ah, through this way, I think, sir, if you don't mind."

He changed direction abruptly at the distant sound of voices. Sloan had almost forgotten the house was still full of people who had paid to see some—but by no means all—of the sights of Ornum House.

"Sometimes," went on the butler, "he would take tea with the family, but more often than not he would be... ah ... absorbed in his work and I would take him a pot to himself in the library."

"I shall want to see the library presently."

"Very good, sir."

"And the ... er ... muniments room."

"Certainly, sir." Dillow had at last reached the door he wanted. He moved forward ahead of them, coughed discreetly, and announced:

"Two members of the county constabulary to see you, milord."

As a way of introducing a country police inspector and his constable, Sloan couldn't have improved on it.

There were two people in the room: a middle-aged man with a long drooping mustache and a pretty woman with fair hair and wide-open eyes of china blue. There was gray now among the fair hair and a rather vague look. The two had obviously just finished afternoon tea and the scene reminded Sloan of a picture he had once seen called Conversation Piece. The only difference as he remembered it was that in the picture the tea had not been drunk. Here, the meal was over, a fact appreciated by Dillow, who immediately began to clear away.

"Bad business," said the Earl of Ornum.

"Yes, sir—milord," Sloan amended hastily. In the nature of things, interviews with the titled did not often come his way.

"Poor, poor Mr. Meredith," said the Countess. "Such a nice man."

Not being altogether certain of how to address a Countess, Sloan turned back to the Earl. "You've seen his sister I understand, milord?"

"No. Tried to. Not at home."

"Oh?"

"House shut up." The Earl pulled gently at one side of his drooping mustache. "She must be away. Accounts for one thing though, doesn't it?"

"What's that, sir—milord?"

"No hue and cry for the man. General alarm not raised. Just chance that that boy—you've got his name, haven't you?"

"Michael Fisher, Paradise Row, Luston," said Constable Crosby, reading aloud from his notebook.

"Just chance that he opened the visor. Otherwise"—the Earl gave another tug at his mustache—"otherwise we might never have found him, what?"

"Possibly not, milord," said Sloan. In fact the late Mr. Meredith might very well have begun to smell very soon, but in a medieval castle there was no knowing to what an unusual noisome aroma might have been attributed.

Drains, suspected Sloan.

"Of course," went on his Lordship, "that suit might have acted like one of those Egyptian things ..."

"Mummy cases?"

"That's it. He might have ... er ... dried up."

"He might," agreed Sloan cautiously. He would ask the pathologist about that. A mummified corpse was certainly one that stood the least risk of being found.

"Should never have thought of looking there for him anyway. Not in a hundred years."

"Quite so," said Sloan. "Now when did you last see Mr. Meredith yourself, milord?"

"Just been talking to m'wife about that. Friday, I thought," he said, adding, "Millicent thinks it was Thursday."

The Countess of Ornum had a high, bell-like voice. "Days are so alike, aren't they, Inspector?"

Sloan said nothing. They might very well be for the aristocracy. They weren't for police inspectors.

"I thought it was Thursday, but it may have been Friday." The Countess looked appealingly round the room as if one or other of the numerous pieces of furniture could tell her.

"I see … er …" Sooner or later the nettle of how to address this vague doll-like woman would have to be grasped. He added firmly, "Milady."

He doubted if she even heard him.

"It isn't," she said, fluttering her eyes at him, "as if anything happened on either day."

"No, milady?"

She smiled. "Then I might have remembered."

It was rather like interviewing cotton wool or blotting paper.

"It would be very helpful, milady," said Sloan formally, "if you could remember."

"I know." She gave him a sweet smile. "I will try. Such a nice man."

"Indeed?" said Sloan, unmoved. It was no great help to him that the deceased had been a nice man.

"Everyone liked him," said the Countess vaguely.

Someone patently hadn't, but Sloan did not say so. Instead he turned back to the Earl. It was easier.

"The pathologist will be here presently, milord, and the police photographers and so forth, after which we will be removing Mr. Meredith to the police mortuary at Berebury."

"Quite so, Inspector." Another tug at the mustache. "Purvis will give you all the help you need. Unless it's a bearer party you want. Then there's Hackle and Dillow and m'nephew."

"Your nephew?"

"Miles. M'brother's boy. Staying with us. Hefty chap."

"And where would I find him?" Sloan would want to interview everybody in time—but especially the hefty.

His Lordship withdrew a watch and chain from his vest pocket. "Silly mid on."

Sloan could hear Crosby snorting by his side. "Where?" he said hastily.

"The cricket field. Playing for Ornum against Petering."

"I see, sir."

"Blood match, you know. Meredith would never have dreamt of missing it ordinarily."

"Keen on the game, was he, milord?"

"Very. That's how he got the job here in the first place."

"Really?"

"Team needed a bowler. M'father took on Meredith."

"As librarian?"

The Earl looked at Sloan. "As a bowler, Inspector. By the time he got past being a bowler no one else knew where to find anything in the library."

"I see, sir." Sloan himself had started as a constable and worked his way up, but things were obviously done differently here. He cleared his throat. "And Lord Cremond, milord? I shall have to have a word with him in due course."

"Henry? He's at the match, too. Scoring."

"Scoring?" That didn't sound right for the son and heir.

"Cut his hand on Friday," said the Earl, "so he couldn't play."

"It was Thursday, I think," said the Countess.

Detective Constable Crosby, who had made a note, crossed it out and then—audibly—reinstated it.

"I'm sorry to hear that," intervened Sloan quickly. "Nothing serious, I hope."

"No, no." The Earl stroked his mustache. "Caught it on some metal somewhere, he said."

"I see, sir. Thank you …"

"I blame myself about Meredith," said the Earl unexpectedly. He had a deep, unaccented staccato voice. "This is what comes of having the house open. I knew no good would come of it in the long run but, you know, Inspector, there's a limit to the amount of retrenchment …"

"Quite so, milord."

"Though what my father would have said about having people in the house for money …"

Sloan prepared to go. "For the record then, Mr. Osborne Meredith was your librarian and archivist, milord?"

"That's right."

The Countess waved a hand vaguely. "He was writing a history of the family, wasn't he, Harry? Such a pity he won't be able to finish it now."

"Yes," said the Earl of Ornum rather shortly.

"My brother's called Harry, too," said Detective Constable Crosby chattily.

Inspector Sloan shot him a ferocious look.

"Mr. Meredith had just made such an interesting discovery," said the Countess of Ornum, undeflected. "He told us all about it last week."

"What was that, milady?" asked Sloan.

The pretty, vague face turned towards him. "He'd just found some papers that he said proved that Harry isn't Earl of Ornum after all."

5

"What was that you said, Sloan?"

Inspector Sloan said louder and more clearly into the telephone, "*Burke's Peerage*, sir, please."

Superintendent Leeyes, still at Berebury Policy Station, grunted. "That's what I thought you said. And is that all you want?"

"For the time being, sir, thank you. I'm expecting Dyson for the photographs any minute now and Dr. Dabbe is on his way over from Kinnisport."

Leeyes grunted again. "And all you want is a *Peerage?*"

"That's right, sir. No ..." Sloan paused. "There is something else, please, now you ask."

"And what may that be?"

"A dictionary."

"A dictionary?"

"Yes, sir. Unless you can tell me what muniments are."

He couldn't.

The two policemen had made their way with difficulty to where the telephone stood. Without the aid of the butler, Dillow, the way had seemed long and tortuous.

And, at one point, doubtful.

That had been when they had turned left and not right by the largest Chinese vase Sloan had ever seen.

"Can't think why they didn't pop the body into that, sir," said Crosby gloomily. "Saved us a lot of trouble, that would."

"There'll have been a reason," murmured Sloan.

That was one thing experience had taught him. There was a reason behind most human actions. Not necessarily sound, of course, but a reason all the same.

"This chap with the cut hand," said Crosby, "we'll have to have a word with him, sir."

"We shall have to have a great many words with a great many people before we're out of here," said Sloan prophetically. "This way, I think ..."

He was wrong. By the time they had taken two more turnings they were lost.

They were in part of the house where the chairs were not roped off with thick red cord, where no drugget lay over the carpet. And on the various pieces of furniture that lined the corridors were small, easily removable ornamental items.

"Do you mind telling me what you are doing here?" It was a thin voice, which seemed to materialize out of the air behind them.

Constable Crosby jumped palpably, and they both spun round.

A very old lady whose skirt practically reached her ankles was regarding them from a doorway. She was hung about with beads, which swung as she talked. Round her sparse gray hair and forehead was a bandeau and her hands were covered in the brown petechiae of arteriosclerotic old age. In her hand was the receiver of a hearing aid, which she held before her in the manner of a radio interviewer.

"You may have paid your half crown, my man, but that does not give you the run of the house."

"Lady Alice?" divined Inspector Sloan.

The thin figure peered a little farther out of the doorway. "Do I know you?"

"No," said Sloan.

"I thought not"—triumphantly—"because I'm not Alice. She's in there."

"Lady Maude?" hazarded Sloan.

She looked him up and down. "That's right. Who are you? And what are you doing here?"

"We've come about Mr. Meredith," said Sloan truthfully.

The beads—by now confused with the wire from the hearing aid to her ear—gave a dangerous lurch to starboard as she shook her head vigorously. "That man! Don't mention his name to me."

"Why not?"

But Lady Maude was not to be drawn.

She retreated into the doorway again. "I never want to see him again."

"You aren't going to," muttered Crosby, sotto voce.

"Not after the things he said." Lady Maude's voice had the variable register of the very deaf. "My sister and I are most upset. He used to take tea with us. We do not propose to invite him again."

The door closed and Sloan and Crosby were left standing in the corridor.

"Dear, dear," said Crosby. "Not to be invited to tea. That would have upset the deceased a lot, I'm sure."

"But not, I fancy, enough to drive him to suicide," murmured Sloan, trying to take his bearings from the corridor.

"It means something though, sir, doesn't it?"

"Oh yes, Constable, it means something all right, but what I couldn't begin to say. Yet."

"No, sir."

"Now to find our way out of here."

"Yes, sir."

"Lead on, Crosby," he said unfairly. "After all, you are a detective constable."

Charles Purvis, steward to the thirteenth Earl of Ornum, had no difficulty in finding his way about the great house and in his turn reported to his superior in much the same way as Sloan had done to his.

"I've arranged for the postmistress to ring us as soon as Miss Meredith gets back to The Old Forge, sir."

His Lordship nodded. "And the boy?"

"Michael Fisher? I took the liberty of slipping him a pound, sir."

"Good. Don't like to think of a man lying dead in the house and us not knowing."

Purvis said, "We'd never have found him."

"No." The Earl waved a hand. "The boy's mother—what happened to her?"

"Mrs. Morley gave her tea and the inspector can see no reason why they shouldn't all go back in the charabanc with the rest of the party."

"Thank God for that," said his Lordship fervently. "The boy sounds a terror."

"He is," said Purvis briefly. "I've just been talking to the coach driver. He's all ready to go, but he's two short."

"Not the boy and his mother?"

"No. A Miss Mavis Palmer and her boyfriend. Last seen three hours ago in the folly."

"Were they?" said the Earl thoughtfully. "Well, get them found, Charles. And quickly. The sooner that particular coachload is off the premises the better. And then come back here. There are one or two other matters which need attending to."

"Yes, sir."

The Earl tugged his left-hand whiskers. "Charles."

"Sir?"

"You'll have the press here by morning."

The young man nodded. "I'd thought of that. Dillow is going to put them in the morning room and then get hold of me as quickly as he can."

"Then there's my cousin and Eleanor."

"Miss Gertrude is still in the china room, sir. I don't think the last of the visitors have quite gone yet. And Lady Eleanor is ... er ... cashing up at the front door."

"They'll both have to be told." The Earl waved a hand. "The house is full of police."

This last was an exaggeration. Inspector Sloan and Constable Crosby had already been swallowed up by the house. And there would, in any case, have been room for the entire Berebury division in the great hall alone.

"Yes, sir," murmured Purvis, who was not paid to contradict the Earl.

"And my aunts."

"We're all right for the moment there, sir. They won't have been out yet. The visitors have hardly gone."

"If I know them," declared Lord Ornum, "they'll be abroad any minute now. On the warpath. Looking for damage."

Purvis moved over towards the window. "We've got a little time anyway, sir. They'll wait until that coach has gone."

The Earl sighed heavily. "And then, Charles, you'd better find out exactly where my nephew William has been all this week."

Purvis hesitated. "I think he's down, sir ..."

The Earl sighed again. "I thought he might be."

"Someone told me that he was in The Ornum Arms last night," said Purvis uneasily.

"Bad news travels fast."

"Yes, sir."

"Then slip down to his cottage and tell him I want to see him, will you, there's a good chap. I think we'd better keep him in the picture in spite of everything."

"Very well, sir."

The Earl lifted an eyebrow. "You don't agree?"

Charles Purvis said carefully, "He's a very talkative young man, sir."

"He gets that from his father."

"Yes, sir, but it might do some harm ..."

"He's my sister's boy, Charles. I can't have him kept in ignorance of trouble here."

"No, sir."

"After all"—a gleam of humor crept into the Earl's melancholy countenance—"we always hear when there's trouble there, don't we?"

"We do indeed," agreed Charles Purvis grimly.

The first of the experts in death had arrived at Ornum House by the time Inspector Sloan and Constable Crosby got back to the armory. They were the two police photographers, Dyson and his assistant, Williams.

Dyson was standing by the door lumbered about with his equipment.

"Nice little place you have here, Inspector."

"And a nice little mystery," rejoined Sloan tartly.

Dyson looked up and down the two rows of armored figures. "Make quite a pretty picture, this will."

"I'm glad to hear it."

"The lab boys will think I've been to the waxworks or something." Dyson walked forward. "Which is the one that didn't get away?"

"Second on the right," said Sloan, "but we'll want some of the total setting, too."

"A pleasure." Dyson assembled his camera and tripod with a rapidity that belied his flippant approach. His assistant handed him something, there was a pause, and then a quick flash. "Don't suppose these chaps have seen anything brighter than that since Agincourt or something."

Sloan was inclined to agree with him. There was an overall gloom about the armory that had nothing to do with the presence of the dead.

Williams, Dyson's assistant, was rigging up some sort of white sheet to one side of the suit of armor for the tilt, circa 1595. He had persuaded Crosby to stand holding one end.

"Need the reflected light," explained Dyson.

Sloan nodded. Dyson never complained about his conditions of work. If he needed anything he brought it with him. He and Williams were self-sufficient members of the police team.

They moved their tripod in front of the suit.

"Inspector?"

"Well?"

"Open or shut?"

"Open *and* shut," said Sloan. "Crosby's done the headpiece for finger-prints."

"Close-helmet," said Dyson.

"What?"

"Close-helmet," repeated Dyson. "That's what it's called. Not head-piece."

"Oh, is it?" said Sloan in neutral tones. "I must remember that."

There was another bright flash. Then Williams moved forward and lifted the visor. Inspector Sloan was surprised again at the sight of the dead face.

"I remember," said Dyson improbably, "when I was an apprentice photographer on the beach at Blackpool, people used to put their faces into a round hole like this …"

"Oh?"

"And we'd take a picture and they'd come up riding on the back of a sea-lion."

"They did, did they?" said Sloan, "Well, let me tell you—"

"Or a camel, sir," interposed Constable Crosby suddenly. He was still holding one end of the sheet. "I've been photographed riding on the back of a camel."

Sloan snapped, "That's enough of—"

"This chap reminds me of that," said Dyson, unperturbed. "Sort of stepping into a set piece, if you know what I mean, Inspector. Just the round face visible."

"I know what you mean. Now get on with it."

"Right-oh."

But for the fact that their subject was dead, the pair of them might have been taking a studio portrait.

"Back a little."

"A bit more to your right, I think."

"What about an inferior angle?"

"Good idea."

"Hold it."

Quite unnecessarily.

"Now a closeup."

"Just one more, don't you think?" Dyson turned. "Anything else, Inspector?"

Sloan grimaced. "I should think the only thing you two haven't done is to ask him to say 'cheese.' "

"No need," said Dyson ghoulishly. "The face muscles contract anyway when you're dead, and you get your facial rictus without asking."

"I see." It was perhaps as well that Dyson had gone in for photography. Knowing all the answers as he did would have got him nowhere on the police ladder of promotion.

Nowhere at all.

"He looks peaceful enough to me," commented Dyson. "Any idea what hit him?"

"Not yet."

"Plenty of weapons to choose from." Dyson made a sweeping gesture that took in the whole collection. "Perhaps it was that one."

"That's a spetum," announced Constable Crosby, who was close enough to read the label.

"A what?" said Sloan.

"Spetum. Honestly, sir."

"Is it indeed?" said Sloan.

"Often confused with a ranseur," added Crosby, straight from the label.

"Well," said Dyson, "I'd rather have that for my money than that nasty-looking piece over there." He indicated a heavy-headed weapon studded with vicious-looking spikes. "What in the name of goodness is that?"

Crosby leaned over and read aloud, "That's a holy water sprinkler."

"Well, I'm blessed," said Dyson, for once strangely appropriate in the phraseology of his reaction. "And the one next to it?"

Crosby moved a step towards a ferocious iron ball on the end of a short chain. "That's called a morning star," he said, "similar to a military flail."

Dyson grinned. "Queer sense of humor the ancients had, didn't they?"

"They did," said Sloan shortly.

Dyson swung his camera back on his shoulder and took the hint. "We'd better be going then." He picked up the heavy tripod. "Williams?"

"Coming."

"Williams." Dyson pointed towards the suit of armor with the wrong end of the tripod. "Williams, it's closing time."

Williams obediently moved forward and lowered the visor and they went.

Dillow put down the heavy silver tea tray.

Presently he would take away the silver teapot (Ann and Paul Bateman, 1792), the hot-water jug (Paul Storr, 1816), and the tray (unknown crafts-man, 1807), clean them and stow them away in green baize in his pantry. For the time being he laid the tray on the kitchen table. Mrs. Morley, the housekeeper, would see to the china (Copeland) and the housemaid would deal with everything else.

Mrs. Morley looked at the butler. "I expect you could do with a cup of tea yourself, Mr. Dillow, after all that fuss and to-do."

He sank into a chair. "That I could, Mrs. Morley, thank you. It's bad enough as it is on open days, but finding Mr. Meredith like that … oh dear, oh dear."

"It's not very nice, I must say." Mrs. Morley pursed her lips. "Dying is one thing—we've all got to go sometime, Mr. Dillow—but dying in a suit of armor …"

Dillow shook his head. Seen close, he was not as old as he seemed at first sight. It was simply that his occupation and bearing gave the impression of age. "I don't like it at all," he said.

"The press will," forecast Mrs. Morley, herself an avid reader of the more sensational Sunday newspapers.

The butler said, "I got quite accustomed to the press in my last position. My late employer ... er ... almost encouraged them. Always offered them a glass of something."

"Ah, Mr. Dillow, but then he was in business."

"Baggles Bearings," said the butler promptly. " 'All industry runs on Baggles Bearings'—that was their advertising slogan. I think they did, too. No money troubles there."

"Business is different," insisted Mrs. Morley.

"Free advertising, that's what he called it every time there was anything in the papers. He used to say even having his art collection mentioned did the bearings a bit of good."

"Well I never," said Mrs. Morley, who could not have said offhand what a bearing was and who knew still less about advertising.

"Mind you," said Dillow ominously, "once they got hold of a story there was no stopping them."

Mrs. Morley looked disapproving. "I don't think his Lordship will favor them mentioning Ornum House."

"They'll rake up everything they can lay their hands on," warned Dillow.

"I'm sure"—stoutly—"there would be nothing that Mr. Meredith would need to hide. There couldn't have been a pleasanter gentleman."

"I wasn't thinking of Mr. Meredith, Mrs. Morley."

The housekeeper looked up quickly. "Master William hasn't been in trouble again, has he?"

"I couldn't say, I'm sure, Mrs. Morley."

Butler and housekeeper exchanged meaningful glances.

Mrs. Morley poured out two cups of tea.

The butler took a sip. "He's down, that's all I know."

"When?"

"I heard he was in The Ornum Arms last night."

Mrs. Morley clucked her disapprobation. "No good ever came out of his going there."

"The police," said Dillow carefully, "are going to want to know when Mr. Meredith was last seen alive."

"Friday," said Mrs. Morley. "You did a tea tray for him in the library."

"So I did," concurred Dillow. "Just after four o'clock."

"Hot buttered toast," said Mrs. Morley, "if you remember. And fruit cake and *petit beurre* biscuits."

"He ate the lot," said Dillow. "There was nothing left when I took his tray."

"When would that have been, Mr. Dillow?"

"About five o'clock."

"And who saw him after that?"

"I couldn't say, Mrs. Morley. I couldn't say at all."

6

Charles Purvis hurried away from the private apartments and slipped easily through the complex layout of the house until he reached the entrance courtyard. Still parked there was a coach. It was painted a particularly raucous blue and, by some irony too deep for words, it was drawn up by the mounting block used by all thirteen Earls of Ornum in the sweep of carriageway where coaches of an entirely different sort had been wont to go into that wide arc of drive that brought them to the front door.

Michael Fisher was standing on the mounting block and the coach driver was sitting peacefully at the wheel of his vehicle with the infinite patience of his tribe. Sooner or later the missing passengers would turn up, lost time could always be made up on the open road, and in any case there was very little point in starting off before opening time. Rather wait here than outside The Fiddler's Delight.

Charles Purvis walked across to the coach to be greeted with excited waves of recognition from Mrs. Fisher.

"Ever so nice, isn't he?" she announced to the assembled coach load, friends and neighbors all, which Purvis was surprised to find annoyed and embarrassed him far more than the deepest insult could have done. "He's what they call the Stooward ..."

He was saved by Michael Fisher doing a sort of war dance on the mounting block.

"Here they come ..."

Purvis turned and everyone in the coach craned their necks to see a slightly disheveled and more than a little flushed Miss Mavis Palmer appear, her boyfriend a few paces behind. There were encouraging shrieks from the entire coachload.

"Come on, Mavis ..."

"Good old Bernard ..."

"Attaboy ..."

The driver started up the engine by way of reprimand to the latecomers—who immediately put on a spurt. Miss Palmer, noted Charles Purvis, outpaced Bernard with ease. He did not begin to contemplate the dance she had doubtless been leading the young man through the park all afternoon, but stood back to let them climb aboard.

With a final burst of cheering and an utterly misplaced fanfare on the coach horn—tally-ho on another sort of coach horn would have been more bearable—the party from Paradise Row, Luston, finally moved away.

Charles Purvis watched for a moment, and then walked across to the doorway.

"Lady Eleanor?"

"Seventeen, eighteen, nineteen …" She turned. "How much is nineteen threepenny pieces?"

"Four and ninepence."

"Are you sure?"

"Er … yes … I think so." He was normally a very sure young man, but Lady Eleanor Cremond was able—with one appealing glance—to convert him into a very uncertain creature indeed.

"That comes right then," she said.

"I don't see how it can," ventured Charles Purvis, greatly daring. "You shouldn't have ninepence at all if you're charging a shilling and half a crown."

She smiled sweetly. "There was a man with one leg …"

"Cut rates?"

"I let him into the park for ninepence. I didn't think he could walk far."

Charles Purvis sat down beside her at the baize-covered table.

"I've really come to tell you something rather unpleasant. Mr. Meredith's been found dead."

"Not Ossy?" she said, distressed. "Oh, the poor little man. I am sorry. When?"

"We don't know when," said Charles Purvis, and told her about the armor.

"But," she protested in bewildered tones, "he didn't even like armor. It was the books and pictures that he loved. And all the old documents."

"I know."

"In fact"—spiritedly—"he wouldn't even show people the armory unless Mr. Ames couldn't come up from the vicarage."

"I know that, too." He began toying with a wad of unused tickets. "When did you last see him yourself?"

She frowned. "Friday afternoon, I think it was."

"You'd better be certain," he warned her. "The police will want to know."

"The police?"

He nodded.

"It was Friday," she said slowly. "Just before tea. I went along to the library and he was there on his own." She hesitated. "He seemed all right then … no … more than all right. Almost exuberant. On top of the world—you know the sort of feeling. Excited, that's it."

"Did he say anything?"

"Say anything? Oh no. I just said I thought he usually took tea with the great aunts on Fridays and he said …" She paused.

"What did he say?"

"He said he thought he had upset them by his discoveries about the earldom."

"And that," said Charles Purvis wryly, "is putting it mildly."

To say that Dillow waylaid those returning from the village cricket match would be an exaggeration and tantamount to unsubtlety on the butler's part.

He simply happened to be hovering in the entrance hall when they happened to return.

"We won," announced Lord Henry as he entered. He was a physical parody of his father, seasoned by his mother's vagueness. "Good match, though."

"I'm very glad to hear it, sir, but—"

"It's a help, of course," chimed in Miles Cremond, close on his heels, "having Henry scoring for us."

"Indeed, sir?"

"Rather." Miles was a square, thickset man with only some of the Cremond family characteristics. His features would blunt badly with time. Already there was a blur where his chin had been. In contrast, his wife, Laura, was a sharp-featured, angular woman, accustomed to command.

"Miles, you should go straight up to change now."

"Yes, dear."

Dillow coughed. "His Lordship has asked to see you all as soon as you came back."

The Earl and Countess were still in their sitting-room. The Earl got to his feet as the three of them trooped in.

"Something wrong, Father?" That was Lord Henry.

"Yes."

Laura Cremond said urgently, "What?"

"Mr. Meredith has met with an accident here."

"Good Lord. Poor chap," said Henry. "I'd no idea he was even in the house."

"Neither," said the Earl of Ornum drily, "had anyone else."

"Didn't think he usually came in at the weekend anyway."

"He didn't."

"Thought it funny he wasn't at the match though," went on Henry. "Haven't known him to miss a match in years."

"Especially the Petering one," put in Miles, fresh from victory.

The Earl of Ornum, aided by several tugs at his mustache, told them about the body in the armor.

Laura Cremond sat down rather suddenly in the nearest chair. "But when did he die?"

"That, Laura, I can't tell you."

Lord Henry said thoughtfully, "Someone wasn't expecting him to be found."

"No," agreed the Earl.

"You couldn't know that that little stinker—what did you say his name was?"

"Michael Fisher."

"Michael Fisher was going to open up Grumpy like that."

"To open up who?"

"Grumpy." Lord Henry gave an engaging smile. "You did say the second suit of armor on the right, didn't you, Father?"

"I did"—heavily.

"That," said his son and heir, "was Grumpy. We called all the suits of armor after Snow White and the Seven Dwarfs, you know, when we were small."

"Did you?"

"Snow White was the puffed and slashed suit," ventured Miles. "Had a feminine touch about it, we thought."

"Indeed?" said the Earl.

"That was the Decadence," said Lord Henry. "We all used to play down there a lot, didn't we, Miles?"

"Oh yes," affirmed Miles. "Cut our milk teeth on the armor, you might say."

"It was Mr. Ames, really," said Lord Henry. "He was such an enthusiast he didn't seem to mind how much we hung about. Taught us a lot."

"All the names for the parts," agreed Miles. "I've forgotten most of them. I expect Henry and William have, too, by now."

"William," the Earl sighed. "I was forgetting William played with you."

Lord Henry frowned in recollection. "There was Dopey, Sleepy, Sneezy—that was the one with the long nosepiece."

"I daresay," said the Earl, "but I don't see—"

"Bascinet," said Miles Cremond suddenly. "I've just remembered—"

"I thought that was something you put a baby in." The Countess of

Ornum, silent until now, came to life like an actress on cue.

"Bascinet," repeated Miles. "That was what Sneezy's helmet was called. A visored bascinet."

"That's right," agreed Lord Henry. "And Dopey's was called a burgonet."

"A closed burgonet," added Miles. "That's what made him look so simple. See, we haven't forgotten after all."

"You do seem to have forgotten that this isn't a nursery game," said his wife sharply.

Miles subsided. "Er … no. Rather not."

"There were seven without Snow White," said Lord Henry consideringly. "I wonder why he ended up in Grumpy?"

"That's easy," said Miles. "Don't you remember, Henry? Grumpy came to pieces easiest."

The Earl's head came up as he said sharply, "Who knew that?"

"Everyone," said Miles helpfully.

Laura Cremond looked round. "Someone put him in there who didn't mean him to be found, I suppose?"

The Earl nodded. "I think so, Laura. And the police want to talk to you all as soon as they can."

After his encounter with Lady Maude, Inspector Sloan found it a positive relief to be talking to a trained specialist.

He met Dr. Dabbe and his assistant, Burns, in the great hall. It hadn't taken the fastest (living) driver in Calleshire long to get from Kinnisport on the coast to Ornum, veering into Berebury to pick up his assistant. His black bag went with him everywhere.

"The weather was just right for sailing," said the doctor reproachfully. "Sunday, too."

Sloan said, "If it had been as warm down there as it is up here, I fancy our chap would have been found a bit sooner."

"Like that, is it?" The pathologist took in the great hall at a glance and followed Sloan down the spiral staircase. Burns brought up the rear.

Dabbe waved his free hand. "Did he walk down here or was he carried?"

"I couldn't say, Doctor. Not yet. I've only seen his face so far."

"I see." Dabbe reached the bottom step. "This the basement?"

"Dungeon level," Sloan corrected him gloomily. After all, this was not a department store. "I don't know if they go lower than this."

"Moat?" suggested Dabbe. "They usually had moats."

Constable Crosby let them into the armory.

"Ah ..." said Dabbe, looking round appreciatively. "Do I take my pick?"

"Second on the right," said Sloan, and not for the first time.

Perhaps he should have put a fresh notice beside the one that was already there. (MAN IN ARMOR, perhaps, or HUMAN REMAINS, CIRCA NOW.)

Aloud he said only, "We've put a chalk ring on the floor, Doctor, round him ... er ... it ..."

"Armor for the tilt, circa 1595," read out the pathologist. "Well, well, well ..."

It wasn't well at all, though Sloan forbore to say so.

"I don't think I've ever seen a corpse ... er ... girded before," said Dabbe.

"No." Neither had Sloan.

The pathologist advanced and looked the armor over. That was one of the things Sloan admired in him. He came, he looked, he examined— then he spoke.

"The deceased?"

"Mr. Osborne Meredith."

"Wasn't a very tall man."

"No," agreed Sloan. The suits of armor—though intimidating—were not large. Both policemen looked down on them without difficulty.

"Too much school milk, that's what it is," said Dr. Dabbe.

"Pardon, Doctor?"

"We're all taller now. People were smaller then." He walked round behind the armor. "It's a pretty complete job. He didn't intend to be stabbed in the back."

Sloan nodded in agreement. From where he was standing it looked as if the man in armor hadn't intended to be stabbed anywhere at all.

"No chinks," said Detective Constable Crosby.

Sloan favored him with a withering stare, and the pathologist's assistant, Burns, who rarely spoke, got out a large thermometer.

"Cold but not damp," observed Dabbe generally.

"Yes," agreed Sloan. It was one of the hottest days of the summer outside, but the heat hadn't penetrated down here. All in all a good place to park a body if you didn't want it found too quickly.

Dabbe was still circling the armor rather as a terrier spoiling for a fight will go round and round his adversary.

"Either, Sloan, they popped him in here pretty smartly after death or else they waited until rigor mortis passed off."

"Oh?"

"Regard the angle of the arms."

Sloan took a fresh look at the man in armor. The boy, Michael Fisher, had said something about the arms.

Dr. Dabbe pointed to—but did not touch—the right arm. It was bent at the elbow in a half defensive position. "He's still on guard."

"Yes, Doctor."

"Before rigor mortis or after. Not during."

"I see."

"After, I expect," said Dabbe mordantly. "By the time you got all this … er … clobber on, it would have begun to set in."

That was another thing to think about. Sloan mentally added it to a very long list of matters to think about. Some of them required action, too, but not until the pathologist had finished. Sloan had been at the game too long not to know that the medical evidence was always of primary importance.

"That's another thing," said Dabbe.

"What is?" Inspector Sloan came back to the present with a jerk.

"How he got into all this."

"Quite so, Doctor."

"And how we're going to get him out." The pathologist gave a fiendish grin. "I can't do a post-mortem with a tin opener."

"No, Doctor."

"Of course," went on Dabbe, "You had an armor-bearer in the old days."

"So you did." Sloan had forgotten that.

"What you might call a body servant, eh, Sloan?" The pathologist's morbid sense of humor was a byword throughout the Berebury Force.

"Quite so"—weakly.

"I shouldn't have said he'd got into this on his own though, even in this servantless day and age," said Dabbe.

"No."

"And I think," said the pathologist, "that we can rule out natural causes, too. Unless coincidence is stretching out a particularly long arm."

"Yes."

"That," said Dabbe cheerfully, "leaves us the usual coroner's trio. Misadventure, suicide, or murder."

"Misadventure?" said Sloan.

"Commonly known, Inspector, as pure bad luck."

"I don't quite see how …"

"The trap for the unwary pathologist, that's what misadventure is," said the doctor feelingly. "Suppose this chap got into this rigout for some perfectly sound reason, and then found he was trapped in it."

"Well?"

"He could have shouted his head off and no one would have heard him through the visor, let alone through the twelve-foot walls they seem to go in for down here."

"That's true, but I don't think he did get into it himself and then call for help, Doctor."

"Oh? Why not?"

"You see, we've checked the floor for footprints. It's all been swept perfectly clean round the armor. Too clean."

"Has it indeed? And what about fingerprints?"

"None of them either. Crosby's been over the lot. The armor's been handled all right—but with gloves on."

The pathologist nodded swiftly. "In that case we can't do a lot of harm by going inside."

He didn't touch the visor, but went straight to the helmet, lifting it with both hands from behind.

There was—after all that—no doubt about how Mr. Osborne Meredith had died.

The back of his skull had been staved in.

7

After he left Lady Eleanor, Charles Purvis went to his car. Ornum House was too far from any of its neighbors to visit them on foot—especially if time was short.

He drove the mile to the village, went through the ornamental gates and out into the High Street. All of the properties there were in good condition, most belonged to the Earl. He nosed his car gently past the usual Sunday afternoon village traffic and stopped outside the last cottage in a row not far from the post office. Most of the village would be watching the cricket, the rest getting ready for evensong. He was quite sure the occupant of number four, Cremond Cottages, would be doing neither.

The man who came to the door was older than both Lord Henry Cremond and Charles Purvis and already running to overweight. He was dressed in old corduroy trousers that were none too clean and a shirt so open-necked as to be undone.

No one could have called his manner agreeable.

"Well, well, if it isn't Charlie-boy."

Purvis stiffened. "Good afternoon, William. Your uncle has sent me down—"

"I didn't think you'd come on your own."

Purvis tightened his lips. "No, I don't think I would."

Suddenly the man grinned. It changed his face completely. "Fifteen all. Your serve—"

"Your uncle sent me down," repeated Purvis stolidly, "to say he wants to see you."

"That's a pleasant change, I must say," drawled William Murton. "I've never known him actually to want to see me before."

"Well, he does now"—shortly.

"Why?"

The steward hesitated. "There's been a spot of trouble up at the house."

"Has there? I'm sorry to hear that." William Murton did not sound particularly sorry. He squinted across the doorway at Charles Purvis. "Someone run off with the family plate, then, or something?"

"Not that sort of trouble."

Murton raised his hands in mock horror. "You don't mean to tell me that some cad has asked for my cousin Eleanor's hand in marriage?"

Charles Purvis flushed to the roots of his hair. "No."

"Not that sort of trouble either?"—offensively.

"No."

"Well, well, how interesting. I shall come at once." He paused on the threshold. "Tell me, does this invitation include a meal, do you suppose?"

"He wants to see you," repeated Purvis.

"I see. What you might call a general summons rather than an invitation."

What Detective Inspector Sloan could have done with was a ball of string.

That was what potholers used when they were in dark caves and wanted to be sure of their way back. It was not unlike that in Ornum House. What he was looking for was the door behind which Lady Maude had retreated earlier on. If he could find a large Chinese vase he thought he would be all right from then on.

He could, of course, easily have asked someone to take him there, but there were risks inherent in the way in which he was announced that might very well disturb the two old ladies with whom he wanted a quiet chat. With whom he wanted a quiet chat before anyone else got to them— which was why he had slipped away from the armory for a few moments.

He was unlucky with the Chinese vase. He found it all right. Vast, well-proportioned, and delicately colored, there was no mistaking it.

Except for one thing.

Its twin.

It wasn't until he had opened a whole series of wrong doors that he realized the gigantic vase he and Crosby had seen had been one of a matching pair. He found the other—the right one—at the far end of the same long corridor. From then on it should have been plain sailing.

He knocked on Lady Maude's door.

A thin old lady—the same one as he had seen earlier—appeared. Fortunately she recognized him.

"I've seen you before."

"That's right, Lady Maude. I wanted to see you again. You and Lady Alice."

"You did?" Sloan felt himself being scrutinized. "Why?"

"Someone has killed Mr. Meredith."

She stared at him for a moment. "Have they indeed. You'd better come in. This way." She turned abruptly on her heel and went back into the room. "Alice, Alice, where are you?"

Lady Alice was—if that were possible—even older than her sister. Old age, however, had not altered the outline of the Cremond nose, which was planted firmly in the middle of a face that in its time must have been striking. Say about the year the Old Queen died.

He stood in front of her. "Good afternoon, your Ladyship."

A clawlike hand lifted a lorgnette and examined him through it in a silence that soon became unnerving. Sloan hadn't felt like that since his early days as a very jejune constable—when he was being checked over by his station sergeant before he was allowed out on the beat. Pencil, notebook, whistle … subconsciously he wanted to make sure that they were all there now.

"Who are you, my man?"

"My name is Sloan, Lady Alice."

"Well?"

Perhaps, conceded Sloan to himself, that hadn't been such a good beginning after all. Circumlocution was a device for handling the middle-aged, not the very old.

"Someone has killed Mr. Meredith."

"Ha!" said Lady Alice enigmatically.

Perhaps, he thought, to the very old death was such a near and constant companion that they minded less.

"And I," he went on, "am a police officer who has come to find out all about it."

Of course, there was always the possibility that she would have expected him to have been in red. The Scarlet Runners, that was what the Bow Street people had been called in their day.

Or should he have just said he was Sir Robert Peel?

"Good riddance," said the old lady vigorously.

He had been wrong to worry about upsetting her then.

"Tryin' to make out that Great-great-great-grandfather Cremond was a bastard."

"Dear me," said Sloan, conscious of the inadequacy of his response.

"Thought the title should have gone to someone else."

"No?"

"Yes," countered Lady Alice firmly. "Said it was all in the archives."

The sooner Superintendent Leeyes sent him that dictionary the better. Then he could find out if archives were the same thing as muniments.

"Always knew it was dangerous to meddle in papers," went on the old lady. "Told m'brother so."

That disposed of the world of scholarship.

"He should have sacked Meredith when he got past cricket."

And sport.

"Always wanted to die in the saddle myself," said the old lady.

Sloan took a second look at Lady Alice. The days of cavalry charges were over, he knew, but in any case surely women had never …

"A good way to go," she said.

Light dawned. Sloan said, "The hunting field …"

"That's right. Now, my man, tell me, who killed him?"

The lorgnette was back again, hovering above the Cremond nose.

"I don't know, Lady Alice."

"He didn't break his neck, did he?"

"No."

"Seen a lot of men go that way. Takin' fences."

Lady Alice had obviously taken her own fences well. At the gallop probably.

Full tilt.

Which brought him back to Osborne Meredith.

Full circle.

"What can you tell me about Friday?" he asked.

Lady Alice might be older, but she was less vague than Millicent, her nephew's wife. "On Fridays Maude and I prepare for Saturday and Sunday."

"Saturday and Sunday?"

"We do not leave our rooms until the evening on Saturdays and Sundays and Wednesdays."

Sloan blinked. He had heard that Mohammedans observed certain rules of behavior between sunup and sundown—but not elderly English spinsters of the Christian persuasion.

"All the year round?" he said tentatively.

With the Mohammedans he understood it was during Ramadan.

"April to October," said Lady Alice.

"And bank holidays," said her sister.

"Except Good Fridays," added Lady Alice.

"I see," said Sloan, who was beginning to …

"My nephew is, of course, head of the family now, but …"

"But what?" prompted Sloan.

"But neither my sister nor I approve of the house being open. What our late brother would have thought we do not like to contemplate."

"Quite," murmured Sloan diplomatically. "So when the house is … er … open, you both remain in your apartments?"

"Always."

It was a pity, that, he thought. Lady Alice and Lady Maude were good value at half a crown.

"Now, about Friday …"

"Yes?"

"Did you see Mr. Meredith at all?"

"No."

"What did you do after tea?"

"What we always do after tea—play ombre."

"Ombre?" One thing was absolutely certain about ombre, whatever it was. You didn't play it for money any more. Inspector Sloan had been a policeman long enough to know all the games you could play for money.

The old lady nodded. "A game our mother taught us."

That took you right back to the nineteenth century for a start. It was the twentieth that Sloan was concerned about.

"Who won?" he asked casually. That was as good a memory test as anything.

He was wrong there.

"Maude," said Lady Alice promptly. "She always wins on Fridays." She waved a thin hand. "It's so much easier that way."

"I see."

"I win on Tuesday, Thursdays, and Saturdays."

"Friday afternoon," he said desperately. "Did you see anyone about on Friday afternoon?"

Lady Alice shook her head. "Just the Judge. And that was much later. As I was going along to dress for dinner."

"The Judge?" Sloan sat up. He really would have to watch his step if there were judges about.

"Judge Cremond," said Lady Alice.

Sloan sighed. Surely there couldn't be more Cremonds still? Purvis hadn't mentioned him in his list of those in the house.

He said, "He's a member of the family, too, I take it?"

"Oh yes." The old lady laughed. "He's a member of the family all right."

"I shall have to interview him in due course, then. I'll make a note of the …"

The old lady's laugh was a cackle now, and not without malice. "I doubt if you'll be able to do that, Mr. Sloan, whoever you are. You wouldn't even see him."

"No?"

"He's been dead these two hundred and fifty years."

"A ghost?" Sloan sighed. There would have to be a ghost, he supposed, in a house like this, but Superintendent Leeyes wouldn't like it all the same.

The lorgnette described an arc in the air on its way towards the Cremond nose. "That's right. Mark my words, young man, someone's going to die soon."

Lady Maude chimed in like a Greek chorus of doom. "The Judge always gets uneasy when someone in the family is going to die."

The Reverend Walter Ames, Vicar of Ornum and Perpetual Curate of Maple-juxta-Handling, was not a preacher of long sermons at any time.

On this particular evening in June he took as his text "unto him that hath shall be given" (a point on which in any case he could seldom think of much to say), said it with celerity, and hurried across from the church to Ornum House.

He reached the armory just as Inspector Sloan got back there.

"I've just heard the sad news," said the vicar somewhat breathlessly. "Terrible. Quite terrible."

"Yes, sir." Inspector Sloan took a quick look round the armory. Dr. Dabbe was engaged in contemplating the armor rather as an inexperienced diner pauses before he makes his first foray into a lobster. Detective Constable Crosby was still prowling round the walls looking at the weaponry.

"I thought something was odd," went on the vicar, who was gray-haired and patently unused to hurrying.

"You did, sir? Why was that?" asked Sloan.

"I blame myself now for not doing more at the time, though I don't see what more …"

"For not doing what?" asked Sloan patiently.

Mr. Ames took a deep breath. "It's like this, Inspector. Meredith sent me a message asking me to come to see him …"

"When would that have been, sir?"

"Friday afternoon. He rang my wife—I was out at the time—and told her that he'd made an important discovery and he wanted my opinion on it."

Sloan looked up quickly. "What sort of discovery, sir?"

The clergyman shook his head. "Ah, he wouldn't say. Not to my wife. And not over the telephone. We … er … still have a … er … manual exchange here in Ornum, you know. Er … a womanual exchange, Inspector, if you take the point."

Sloan did.

"He just left a message with my wife," went on the vicar, "asking me to come up to the house."

"And did you, sir?"

"Oh yes, Inspector. That was what was so odd."

"What was so odd?"

"When I got here I couldn't find him."

"What time would that have been, sir?" It was, Sloan thought, for all the world like a catechism.

"About half-past five. He told my wife he would be working in the muniments room after tea, and that I would find him there. But I didn't."

"What did you do then?"

"Glanced in the library—I didn't see him there either—and came away again."

"Then what?"

"I decided I'd missed him after all and that I'd call at The Old Forge on my way back to the vicarage. Which I did."

"But he wasn't there," agreed Sloan.

"Quite so. No reply at The Old Forge." The vicar averted his eyes from the armor. "At the time I thought I would be seeing him at the cricket on the Saturday and Sunday—a two-day match, you know, the Ornum versus Petering one—so I didn't go back to his house again."

"But he wasn't at the cricket," persisted Sloan.

"No," admitted Mr. Ames. "I must confess I was surprised about that—though it is now painfully clear why he wasn't there."

"Did you do anything more?"

The vicar shook his head. "I'm afraid not. I realize now that I should have done, but it rather slipped my mind." He looked round at Dr. Dabbe, his silent assistant, Burns, and Constable Crosby, and said apologetically, "I fear that I underestimated the importance of poor Meredith's discovery—whatever it was."

Sloan nodded. "I daresay you did, sir."

"Meredith often got excited about his work, you know, Inspector." Clearly this was going to take a good deal of expiation on the vicar's part.

"I understand, sir. You thought he was crying wolf."

"I think"—very fairly—"that we all tend to exaggerate what is important to us and to diminish what others regard as important."

But it was after all that that Mr. Ames really began to assist the police in their enquiries.

Not in the usual sense.

"I thought that this would be the particular suit of armor," he said, "as soon as I heard about the tragedy."

"Why?" demanded Sloan sharply.

"It disarticulates more easily than the others."

"You don't say," murmured Dr. Dabbe, who hadn't yet been able to disarticulate it at all.

"Who all would know that?" asked Sloan.

"Everyone," said the vicar blithely. "It's the one I demonstrate on when people come. A most interesting piece if I may say so. Poor Meredith. A real expert in his own field, you know."

"It's a question of the post-mortem, Vicar," intervened Dr. Dabbe, anxious to get on in his own line of expertise.

"Quite so. Now, you've got the skull off, I see."

Someone had also almost got Meredith's skull off, too, and Mr. Ames winced visibly at the sight.

"Yes," agreed Dabbe, "but that's not enough for the coroner."

"Of course not." Mr. Ames nodded rapidly. "What you want to do is to get down to the … er … ah … um …"

"Body," said Dabbe.

"Ere … quite so. Well, it's not difficult."

"Can I get this off for a start?" asked the doctor.

"The pauldron? Only if you remove the besaque …"

Detective Inspector Sloan motioned to Crosby and they both stood aside for a few moments, the better to relish the edifying situation of someone using long words that the doctor did not understand.

Dr. Dabbe leaned forward and caught his sleeve on a protruding hook as he did so. He swore under his breath.

"Ah, you've found the lance rest then, Doctor." That was Mr. Ames.

"Let us say," murmured the pathologist pleasantly, "rather that it found me."

"Perhaps it might be as well to start with the gauntlets and couters. Then we can get the vambraces off."

"That will be a great help, I'm sure."

"Well, you'll be able to see the hands and forearms," said the vicar practically, "but the breastplate and the corsets are really what …"

"I beg your pardon?"

"The breastplate and corsets …"

"Corsets?"

"That's right."

"So that's where it all began …"

"The corselet was a sort of half-armor," explained Mr. Ames academically, "but these are true corsets."

"Well, well, well …"

"Made in pairs, usually hinged, and tailored to fit."

"You don't say. And that?"

The vicar coughed. "The codpiece, and now"—hastily—"to get the gorget off ..."

The figure of an elderly man in a dark gray suit was beginning to emerge.

Blood had run down the back of the neck and onto the collar and suit, and had dried there.

As the vicar deftly loosened the corset, the body started to keel over.

8

Drawn together by the unexpected, the family had stayed together in a group in the sitting room of the private apartments. They were still there when Charles Purvis got back from Ornum village with William Murton.

Murton made a little mock bow towards them.

"You wanted to see me?" he said. There was the faintest of ironic stresses on the word "wanted."

"Thought we'd better put you in the picture, William," the Earl said gruffly. "Something of a mishap …"

"Yes?"

"Meredith's been found dead in the armory …"

"In a suit of armor, actually," added Lord Henry quickly. "In the suit we called Grumpy. Do you remember Grumpy?"

William Murton nodded. "I remember Grumpy all right." He frowned. "Second on the right on the way in."

"That's right," said the Earl heavily.

There was a slight pause, then:

"Poor Ossy," said William. William Murton was a strange admixture of physical characteristics. He was heavier than the Cremonds but he, too, had the Cremond nose. With it, though, he had a flamboyance of manner missing in the others. "Somebody put him there, I take it?"

"Quite so," said the Earl.

"When?"

"Nobody seems to have seen him since Friday."

"I came down on Friday," said William, "seeing as you probably don't like to ask."

"When on Friday?" said Laura Cremond harshly.

William turned towards her with an expressionless face. "In the afternoon, Laura. When did you come down?"

She flushed. "Thursday."

"We came down for the match," mumbled Miles.

"Match?" said William Murton, looking round at everybody. "Match?"

"You know," said Miles eagerly. "Ornum versus Petering."

"Tiddledywinks?"

70

"Cricket."

Laura Cremond said, "He's teasing you, Miles."

"Cricket," said William, slapping his thigh. "Of course. That reminds me—I had some money on that."

Miles stared at him. "Money on a cricket match?"

"That's right, old boy."

"But people never …"

"Gents don't," said William. "People do. Who won?"

"We did."

"Good. Thought you would. Old Lambert owes me a fiver then."

"Ebeneezer Lambert never backed a winner in his life," observed the Earl sadly. "Same in my father's day. Poor judge of horses."

"And men," said William.

"Men?"

"He was a friend of my father's, you know."

"Quite so," said the Earl.

"You could have almost called them colleagues," went on William bitterly, "seeing how Lambert was a saddler and my father was a groom."

"Quite so," said the Earl again.

"Only colleague isn't quite the right word when it comes to following a trade, is it?"

"Craft," said the Earl mildly. "You worry too much about the past, William. It's all over now."

"Me worry about the past? I like that! You've all got a full-time man here doing nothing much else except poke about into family history. And if that isn't worrying about the past I don't know what is."

"Only we haven't got him any more," said Lord Henry diffidently, "have we?"

William turned towards his cousin. "No more you have. Met with a nasty accident, did he?"

"So it would seem," said Henry. "The police are down in the armory now. Then they want to see us all."

"It's a pity," observed William to no one in particular, "that it should happen just when Ossy was getting on so well, isn't it?"

"Very."

"Or was I misinformed?"

"No."

"There are those," added Murton meaningfully, "who might say that meddling with the past is downright dangerous, aren't there?"

"There are," agreed Lord Henry, "and who's to say they aren't right?"

Alone of the rest of the family Miss Gertrude Cremond was not in the sitting-room. She was still presiding over the room devoted to the display of fine china.

Detective Inspector Sloan found her there by the simple process of following the route that the public took through the house. It was, he decided, rather like playing one of those games based on the maze principle. Each time he came to a dead end—in this case either a locked door or a thick, looped cord—he went back two paces and cast about in another direction.

Eventually he came to the china. It looked very beautiful in the long light of an early summer evening—which was more than could have been said for Miss Gertrude Cremond. She was shorter and squarer than the Earl, but still unmistakably a Cremond.

She had the nose.

She could not remember when she had last seen Osborne Meredith alive.

"He wasn't really interested in the china, Inspector. Not as an expert, I mean."

"I see, miss, thank you." Some unmarried ladies Sloan called "miss," some he called "madam." There was a fine distinction between the two, which he wouldn't have cared to have put into words and had nothing to do with age.

"But if I can help you at all in any other way …" said Miss Cremond.

"You deal with the china yourself, do you?"

"All of it," she agreed. "And the flowers. Lady Eleanor helps me with the flowers when she is at home. As a rule we do those on Tuesdays and Fridays. We have fresh flowers in all the public rooms when the house is open."

"Fridays you'll be busy," he said.

"Always."

"This last Friday, can you remember what you did in the afternoon?"

"The great hall chandelier," responded Miss Cremond promptly. "It took a long time—in fact I came back after tea to finish it off. You must have it hung back if the public are to be admitted. It would soon get broken if not."

"Quite so, miss. And afterwards?"

She frowned. "It took me until it was time to change. Dillow hung it after dinner."

"I see, miss, thank you." He paused. "If you should remember noticing anything at all unusual about Friday evening I should be glad to be told."

"Of course, Inspector."

Sloan began to go. "Lady Alice tells me that she saw Judge Cremond on Friday evening."

Subconsciously he had expected a light laugh and an apology for an eccentric old lady. What he got was:

"Oh, dear." And a worried look came over Miss Gertrude Cremond's plain face. "That's a bad sign, I must say."

"Well, Sloan?"

Sloan was back on the telephone to Berebury police headquarters.

"Dr. Dabbe has had a look at the body now, sir "

Superintendent Leeyes grunted. "Well?"

"Depressed fracture, base of skull."

"Not suicide then."

"No, sir. Not accident either. Not unless someone popped the lid—I mean, the helmet—back on again afterwards, stood him in the right place, and dusted the floor all round."

"Murder then."

"I'm afraid so. Hit," said Sloan pithily, "very hard on the back of the head with an instrument which may or may not have been blunt."

"I suppose," rejoined Superintendent Leeyes, "that we could have expected the traditional at Ornum."

"Yes, sir. As to what did it …"

"If you mean weapon, Sloan, for heaven's sake say so."

Sloan coughed. "We're a bit spoilt by choice for weapons, sir."

"Are you?"

"There are one hundred and seventy-seven, sir, not counting two small cannon at the front door."

"I don't think"—nastily—"we need count the cannon, do you, Sloan?"

"No, sir."

"What other sort of weapons do you have … er … on hand?"

Sloan took a deep breath. "What you might call assorted, sir. Very. Everything from a poleaxe to a partisan."

"A what?"

"A partisan, sir. Of blued steel." Sloan hesitated. Offering information to the superintendent could be a tricky business. "It's like a halberd."

"Is it, Sloan?"—dangerously. The only partisans known to the superintendent were his enemies on the watch committee. (The only place, if it came to that, where there was a resistance movement.) "I take it that a halberd is like a partisan?"

"No, sir—I mean, yes, sir."

"Then you'd better find out exactly which one it was that killed him, hadn't you?"

"Yes, sir." He cleared his throat. "Constable Crosby's started going through the catalogue now."

"Catalogue?" echoed Leeyes. "And do you propose, Sloan, looking the murderer up in *Who's Who* or some such similar publication?"

"No, sir"—patiently. "A catalogue of the weapons was made by the vicar, a Mr. Walter Ames, who's something of an authority on arms and armor."

"Is he indeed?"

"And Crosby's going through it now."

"I see."

"The trouble, sir, is that the family's been armigerous ..."

"Been what?"

"Armigerous."

"Where did you get that word?"

"The doctor used it, sir."

"That," said Leeyes severely, "doesn't mean you should."

"It's a heraldic term, sir, not a medical one. It means the Ornums have been entitled to bear arms for a very long time. Like"—suddenly—"like police are allowed to carry truncheons."

It was not a happy simile.

"Truncheons," said Leeyes trenchantly. "What have truncheons got to do with it?"

"They are weapons we're entitled to carry, sir. In the same way the Ornums were entitled to bear arms in the old days. That's why there is so much of it about in the armory—to say nothing of the fact that the twelfth Earl was a great collector."

"It seems to me," said his superior officer pontifically, "that you are confusing arms with weapons. It's a weapon you want, Sloan. And quickly."

"Yes, sir."

"What other long words did the doctor use?"

"He said he thought the deceased had been dead for roughly forty-eight hours."

"Friday."

"Yes, sir."

"No one saw him alive on Saturday, I suppose?" The superintendent had no more faith in medical than in any other considered opinion.

"Not that I've heard about," said Sloan carefully. "Teatime on Friday seems to have been the last occasion he was seen."

"And how long had he been in the armor?"

"Dr. Dabbe couldn't say, sir, but he thought he hadn't been put into it until after rigor mortis had passed off."

"That means the body must have been parked somewhere, Sloan."

"Or just left, sir, where it was killed."

"Where was that?"

"I don't know, sir. Not yet. It's big house."

"Not," sarcastically, "a room for every day of the year?"

"Not quite, sir, but ..."

"But you haven't quite mastered the geography yet, eh, Sloan? Is that it?"

That was one way of putting it.

Not a way Sloan himself would have chosen, but Superintendent Leeyes was not a man with whom to argue.

Instead of arguing Sloan said formally, "I have already interviewed some of those persons present in the house and warned them that I shall wish to talk to them again . ."

A noncommittal grunt came down the line.

"I have also instigated enquiries about the present whereabouts of the deceased's sister and am endeavouring to establish who was the last person to see him alive ..."

"The last but one will do nicely for the time being, Sloan."

"Yes, sir."

"These people in the house ..."

"The Ornums and their servants, sir."

"I see. That's the Earl ..."

"And his wife, his cousin, his two aunts on his father's side, his son and his daughter, his nephew, and his nephew's wife."

"Ha! The extended family, Sloan." The superintendent had once read a book on sociology and felt he had mastered that tricky discipline.

"I beg your pardon, sir?"

"Nothing, Sloan. Just a technical term."

"I see, sir. There is also an additional nephew."

"Oh?"

"A Mr. William Murton."

"Makes a change from Cremond, I suppose," observed Leeyes.

"His mother was a Cremond. She married a groom."

"She did what?" The superintendent, who dealt daily with sudden death, larceny, road traffic accidents, and generally saw the seamy side of human nature, was not easily shocked, but there were some things ...

"She ran away with her groom," said Sloan. "Mr. William Murton, the Earl's nephew, is the outcome of the union."

"And where does he come in?"

"I couldn't say, sir. Not yet. He has a cottage in Ornum village which he uses—mostly at weekends. The rest of the time he lives in London. I understand he paints."

The superintendent didn't like that.

"And," pursued Sloan, "there is also the Earl's steward, a man called Charles Purvis. He lives in a little house in the park and comes all over a twitter whenever he looks at young Lady Eleanor."

"Like that, is she?"

"No, sir"—repressively—"she is not. Apart," he went on, "from this … er … one big happy family"—Sloan didn't know if this was the same thing as an extended one or not—"there are the servants."

"Loyal to the core, I suppose?"

"Well …"

"Above suspicion?"

That was not a term Sloan had been taught to use.

"Trusted to the hilt, then," suggested Leeyes, who in his youth had been grounded in heroic fiction.

"No …"

"Been with them all their lives?" The superintendent was rapidly running out of phrases associated with family servants.

"No, sir. Oddly enough, not. The cook has. Started as a tweeny at twelve and worked her way up, but the housekeeper has only been there a couple of years and the butler rather less. About eighteen months. The other girl—I don't know what you'd call her …"

"I'd call her maid-of-all work," said Leeyes promptly.

"She's been with them about three years. That's the indoor staff. Outside there are two men and a boy looking after the park and gardens. One of them—Albert Hackle—comes in on open days to show off the dungeons."

"Perhaps," said Leeyes, "there'll be someone in them soon."

Sloan said sedately that he would see what he could do and rang off.

What he wanted to do next was to find the parts of the house where Osborne Meredith had spent his working time. The library and the muniments room.

Stepping away from the telephone, he met Lord Henry. He asked the young man to lead him to the rooms.

He wished he had gone there sooner.

The library was apparently in perfect order.

The muniments room looked as if it had been hit by a tornado.

9

Detective Inspector Sloan didn't step very far into the muniments room.

Just far enough to see that the disarray was not that left by an exceptionally untidy scholar.

It was not.

From where he stood he could see that it had been carefully calculated. Sheets of manuscripts lay disarranged on the floor, documents of every sort were strewn all over the place. A great chest lay open, its contents distributed far and wide.

"Phew!" whistled Lord Henry over Sloan's shoulder.

"Don't come any farther, my lord," warned Sloan. "I'll need to take a proper look round the room first."

"It's a bit of a mess."

"Quite so."

Typical English understatement, that was. Sloan's gaze swept the room and noted that the disturbance had every appearance of being systematic. It looked as if every drawer had been opened, every deed unrolled. Long scrolls of paper covered all the surfaces, and, sprinkled over everything like some monstrous oversize confetti, were dozens and dozens of filing cards.

"Poor Ossy," murmured Lord Henry quietly. "I hope he didn't see this. A more orderly man didn't exist."

"Those filing cards …"

"All the deeds, documents, and depositions," said Lord Henry, "recorded and cross-referenced. It took him years."

Sloan nodded. "The room was never locked?"

"No. This part of the house isn't ever shown to the public." Lord Henry was still looking at the room as best he could round the police inspector. "That's a funny thing, though."

"What is, my lord?"

"The room isn't kept locked, but the document chests always were."

Together they peered at the iron-banded chests. Keys were clearly visibly from where they stood, still in the locks.

"Who had the keys to them?" asked Sloan automatically.

"Just my father and Ossy."

"I see." Sloan made a mental note about that. The contents of the deceased's pockets would be recorded by the police in due course. Just at the moment they were inviolate behind a portion of armor called a tasset.

Lord Henry frowned. "Ossy would never have left them open like that—or even with the keys in. They're much too important for that."

"He might not have had the choice," Sloan reminded him.

"No, of course not. I was forgetting." Lord Henry's gaze rested on the disheveled room. "There's another extraordinary thing, Inspector, isn't there?"

"What, my lord?"

"All this confusion ..."

"But no actual damage."

This was quite true. Disorder reigned supreme, but none of the papers appeared to be torn or defaced.

"Just as if someone only wanted a muddle," said his Lordship perceptively.

"These documents must have value," began Sloan. "It stands to reason ..."

"To an antiquarian perhaps, Inspector. But not an intrinsic value like the pictures or the books or the china."

Sloan shifted his weight from one foot to the other. "If there was anything missing ..."

Lord Henry said carefully, "Then only Ossy would be able to tell you."

"And he can't do that now."

"No." The younger man paused. "Moreover, Inspector, if he were here to tell us, it would take him a very long time indeed to put this room to rights—even though we may think nothing's been damaged. Months. Years, perhaps."

Sloan could see that for himself.

"Presumably," he said, going on from there in his mind and thinking aloud, "this room would otherwise have told us something useful."

"But what?" asked Lord Henry, surveying the muddled muniments from the door.

Sloan decided that their message—if any—would have to wait for the time being.

He turned his scrutiny to the floor. There was no blood immediately visible. Mr. Osborne Meredith did not appear to have been killed here. And whoever had created this disturbance had been careful not to stand on any of the papers.

Or had they?

Sloan dropped to his knees and looked along at ground level. There was an imprint of sorts on one piece of paper.

A heel mark.

A heel mark so small and square that it must have come from a woman's shoe.

Detective Constable Crosby was asking Charles Purvis the Earl's name.

He did not know it, but this—like matrimony—was not something to be taken in hand lightly.

"It's for the coroner," he began. "I need to know the full name of the occupant of the premises in which the deceased is presumed to have met his death."

"The full name?" said Charles Purvis dubiously.

"The full name."

"Henry," said the steward. "The eldest son is always called Henry." Crosby wrote that down.

"Augustus." After the Duke of Cumberland—or was it the Roman General?

Crosby wrote that down too.

"Rudolfo."

"Rudolfo?"

"The tenth Earl was invested with a foreign order. He was the English ambassador to the country at an awkward time diplomatically and ... er ... carried it off well. Saved the situation, you might say. He called his own son after their reigning monarch of the day—that went down well, too. The name has been kept."

"I see," said Constable Crosby laconically. "That the lot?"

Purvis stiffened. "By no means. There's Cremond, too."

"That's the surname, isn't it?"

"As well."

"As well as what?"

"As well as being a Christian name."

Crosby wasn't sure what Purvis meant and said so.

"Twice," said Charles Purvis.

"You mean he was christened Cremond as well as having it as a sur-name."

"That's right."

"Cremond," Crosby looked incredulous, "and Cremond?"

The steward coughed. "That dates back to the middle of the eighteenth century when ..."

Crosby wasn't listening. "William Edward Crosby Crosby," he said under his breath, for size.

"I beg your pardon, Constable?"

Crosby turned back to his notebook, and read aloud, "Henry Augustus Rudolfo Cremond Cremond?"

Name of a name of a name, that was …

"That's right," agreed the steward and comptroller. "Thirteenth Earl Ornum of Ornum in the County of Calleshire, Baron Cremond of Petering …"

"There isn't," said Detective Constable William Edward Crosby of 24 Hillview Terrace, Berebury, with tremendous dignity, "any room on the form for that."

Sloan methodically sealed the door of the muniments room and went back next door to the library. This was a very fine room.

It was divided into six small bays all lined with books—three bays on either side of the center. The right-hand three each ended in a window and a window seat with a view over the park. The left-hand three consisted entirely of bookshelves with a sliver of table down the middle. At the far end was a bust of Lord Henry.

"My great-great-grandfather," murmured Lord Henry.

Sloan shot a swift glance from the bust of Lord Henry and back again. There was no discernible difference between the two.

"Army," said Lord Henry by way of explanation. "Too young for Waterloo. Too old for the Crimea."

Sloan advanced. Apart from the neckwear, the bust might just as well have been Lord Henry. It was as near a replica as he'd seen.

"Mr. Meredith worked here, too, I take it," he said generally.

Lord Henry nodded. "Spent nearly all his time between the library and the muniments, though he was always popping down to have a look at the pictures, too."

"As to Friday," said Sloan, "if he'd been working here then, what sort of traces would you have expected to find?"

"None," said his Lordship promptly. "He wasn't that sort of scholar. When he'd finished with a book, he'd put it back in its right place."

Sloan wasn't surprised. From what little he'd seen of the body that had emerged pupa-like from the chrysalis of the armor, he'd have said Meredith was a neat, dapper little man.

Lord Henry carried on, "He was quite mild about everything else, but it was as much as your life was worth to spoil the order on the bookshelves."

This wasn't perhaps the happiest of comparisons, and Lord Henry's voice trailed away.

"I see," said Sloan, moving down the three bays.

Everything was utterly neat and tidy. At the end by the door a small stack of papers on the table there was the only testimony that the room had ever been used at all. The first two bays seemed normal enough. Sloan paused at the third.

The casual observer—the untrained eye—would probably have seen nothing.

Sloan did.

What he saw was on the spine of Volume XXIV of *The Transactions of the Calleshire Society*.

Blood.

This, then, was in all probability where the librarian and archivist to the Ornum family had met his death.

Sloan stepped carefully round the thin table and measured a few distances with his eye. The photographers would have to come back and bring the lab boys with them. In the meantime …

At a quick guess the deceased could have been sitting at the inside end of the table, which ran the length of the bay. He had been hit from behind—the pathologist had told him that much—and from above. The height of the book with the blood on it confirmed that.

Lord Henry cleared his throat. "This the spot, then?"

"I think so," said Sloan. There was nothing much else to point to it. The table might have had blood on it and been wiped clean. There might be drops on the floor. The library carpet was Turkey red, which didn't help … and any derangement of chair and table had long ago been made good. And marks of scuffed heels on the pile of the carpet would have …

"The cleaning arrangements in here …" began Sloan.

But he had asked the wrong man.

"Not really my department," said his young Lordship frankly. "Dillow will know."

"I see," said Sloan. He wouldn't mind another word with the butler. "Where would I find him now?"

"It's easier than that." Lord Henry drifted across the library and tugged at a green silk sash. "He'll find us."

It was, in fact, simplicity itself.

"Thank you." Sloan wasn't sure about the paths of righteousness, but those of some people could be made very smooth indeed. He cleared his throat. "By the way, my lord, your injury …"

"Silly thing to do." Lord Henry's bandaged hand was still drooping down like a limping dog's paw. "I cut it on Friday morning fiddling about with my car."

"Were you alone at the time?" enquired Sloan pertinently.

"Oh yes, Inspector. Nobody else here really cares about cars. I caught it between the fan blade and the engine."

"I see."

"Trying to tune her up a bit and all that …"

The library door opened. "You rang, my lord?"

"Ah, Dillow, the inspector wants another word with you."

The butler, professionally expressionless, turned expectantly to Sloan.

"Friday," said Sloan. "Friday afternoon. You said you brought Mr. Meredith his tea here."

"That is correct, sir. At four o'clock. I collected the empty tray a few minutes before five."

"Did you see Mr. Meredith then?"

"Not the second time, sir. The tray was on the table by the door and I just collected it …" The man hesitated. "In fact, sir, I'm afraid I assumed Mr. Meredith had gone home because the vicar called about half an hour later, asking for him, and he said he'd tried the muniments room and he wasn't there. I took the liberty of telling him that Mr. Meredith must have gone home then, though of course I realize now that …"

"Quite so," said Sloan. "And after that?"

"After, sir?"

"When did you next come in here?"

Dillow frowned. "Yesterday morning sometime, sir, it would have been. Just to see that the room had been put to rights. Though Mr. Meredith was such a tidy gentleman that I knew nothing would need doing."

"And did it?"

"No, sir, not that I recollect."

"Whose job is it to see that the room had been tidied?"

"Mine, sir, to see it had been done. Edith's to … er … do it."

"Edith's?" The nuances of the division of labor among domestic staff were lost on Sloan. Now if it had been police work …

"She's the housemaid, sir, but …"

"Yes?"

"On open days, sir, we all tend to devote ourselves to the rooms which are shown."

"I see. And the muniments room?"

"I didn't go in there, sir, at all. Mr. Meredith liked to deal with that himself. It's a small room and when any cleaning was done in there Mr. Meredith always arranged to be present himself so that nothing was disturbed."

"The muniments room? Turned upside down? Look out, Dillow, you're spilling that soup."

"I beg your pardon, my lord."

"I should think so. Henry, who the devil would want to play about in the muniments room of all places? Nobody ever goes in there."

"Couldn't say," said the son and heir. "But somebody has ... er ... did. And you can't go and see because the inspector has sealed it up. And the library."

The dining room at Ornum House that evening was scarcely more festive than the armory. The Earl of Ornum sat at one end of the table, the Countess at the other. Ranged round the table were the rest of the family.

Dillow hovered.

William Murton, whose summons to Ornum House had, in fact, gone on to include a meal, took an immediate interest. "That means something, doesn't it? I mean, you wouldn't go to the bother of stirring up the papers without a reason, would you?"

"I wouldn't," responded Henry.

"But," asked Laura Cremond, "what was there in there that mattered anyway?"

"Search me," said Lord Henry frankly. "Never could make head or tail of those papers myself. All that cramped writing. In Latin, too, most of it. Still, I expect it meant something ..."

"Your inheritance," said his father drily.

"It must have meant something to somebody else, too," pointed out Miles Cremond, who always followed his wife's conversational leads. "Else they wouldn't have messed it about."

Cousin Gertrude, who was a considerable trencherwoman, looked up from a bit of steady eating and said, "Does that mean that now no one can prove that Harry here isn't Earl of Ornum?"

There was a small silence.

The Earl of Ornum crumbled some bread and wondered why it was that plain women so often went in for plain speaking.

"Well," demanded Gertrude Cremond, "can they or can't they?"

Millicent, Countess of Ornum, was always equal to a straight question.

"Poor Mr. Meredith," she said tangently, "to be killed *and* to have his work spoilt like that ..."

"Ossa on Pelion," murmured Lord Henry, upon whose education a great deal of money had been expended.

"Too terrible," said the Countess.

"To be killed by someone he knew," observed her daughter quietly.

"Eleanor! Surely not."

"Unless some total stranger happened to walk in, take a dislike to his face, and kill him."

"But," protested Millicent Ornum, "he had a nice face. Crinkled but pleasant. Not the sort of face you'd take a sudden dislike to at all."

Eleanor sighed. "Exactly, Mother."

"So it wasn't his face," drawled William Murton.

"It must have been something else then, what?" said Miles Cremond with the air of one reaching a studied conclusion.

"Yes, Miles," said Lord Henry kindly. "We think it was."

"So if Ossy's dead and the papers are all messed up then no one can prove anything?"

"A veritable nutshell, old chap. There's just the one small point …"

"What's that?"

"Who did for Ossy."

A baffled look came over Miles Cremond's face. "Yes, of course."

"It's no use our pretending," said Cousin Gertrude bluntly, "that it doesn't make any difference to any of us whether Harry here is Earl of Ornum because it does." She looked round the table. "To every single one of us."

There was a chorus of protest.

"Yes, it does," insisted Gertrude. "Henry here'll kill himself one day in that sports car of his. Always trying to make it go faster and faster."

"I say, Cousin Gertrude, steady on."

"That means Miles would come in to the title and you can't tell me that wouldn't please Laura."

Laura Cremond's thin face went a sudden pink. "Really, Gertrude, I don't think that remark is in the best of taste."

"Neither is murder."

"Are you suggesting that Miles and I killed Mr. Meredith?"

Gertrude Cremond was equal to a frontal attack. Not for nothing had she stood foursquare against the opposing center forward on the hockey field. "No," she said, "but you were both late for dinner on Friday evening, weren't you?"

"Well, I must say that sounds remarkably like an insinuation to me."

"Merely an observation," remarked Cousin Gertrude, unperturbed. "Why were you both so late?"

"Miles went for a walk and I waited for him to get back before I came down. That's why."

"Did you go for a walk, Miles?"

"What? Oh, me? Yes, rather."

"Where?"

"Where? Oh—in the park, you know. Actually I went round the ha ha.

To get in training for the match, what? No exercise to speak of in town, don't you know."

"Never touch it myself," said William Murton, looking with close interest from one flushed face to the next.

"Touch what?" said Miles.

"Exercise." William patted his tummy. "Went to seed early myself. Less trouble."

Cousin Gertrude rounded on him as if he'd been a wing half coming up fast on the outside. "There's no need for you to talk, William. You'd miss your uncle Harry here more than anyone."

"True."

"You may not touch exercise," she went on tartly, "but you're certainly not above touching him for money when you need it."

"Granted." He made a mock bow in her direction. "But you will be pleased to hear I've turned over a new leaf. My ... er ... touching days are gone."

This produced total silence. The Earl and his son exchanged a quick glance.

"Truly," said William. "I haven't asked you for a loan this trip, Uncle Harry, now have I?"

"Not yet," said that peer cautiously.

Cousin Gertrude was inexorable. "Moreover," she went on, "there's the Judge taking to walking about again. I hear that Aunt Alice saw him on Friday evening. You all know what that means."

There was an immediate chorus from Eleanor, Henry, Miles, and William. "Someone's going to go!"

Laura Cremond turned on her husband. "Really, Miles ..."

"Sorry, dear, learned the responses as a child."

"You are now a grown-up."

"Yes, dear."

"I don't think," said Gertrude astringently, "that Laura quite appreciates that the Judge being seen always means that someone is going to die."

"He's dead," insisted Laura. "You've all been saying so."

"Not Ossy. He doesn't count. It's got to be a member of the family," declared Gertrude.

"It's a family legend," said William Murton, adding ironically, "You needn't worry, Laura. It only applies to blood relations."

"Like the two black owls and the Duke of Dorset in *Zulieka Dobson*," explained Lord Henry swiftly. Laura was looking cross.

"And the dying gooseberry bush in the walls of Kilravock Castle," added Lady Eleanor.

"And just as true," insisted Miss Cremond.

"Never mind, Cousin Gertrude," said Lord Henry helpfully. "Perhaps it's one of the great-aunts. After all, they are knocking ninety and they can't live forever, you know."

"Talking of the aunts," said Eleanor suddenly, "where are they tonight?"

"They've taken umbrage," said her brother.

"Why?"

"Mother used Great Aunt Maude's hearing aid as a pepper pot last night."

"No …"

"It's a fact," said Lord Henry. "Poor old Maude. She stood it on the table all the better to hear with and Mother started shaking it all over her soup."

"It is a bit like one, you know," murmured Millicent Ornum defensively, "until you look at it closely."

But Cousin Gertrude had not done.

Heated and anxious, she said, "Don't you all realize that somebody we know killed poor Ossy?"

There was silence.

"Someone here in Ornum House," she said. "Perhaps someone in this very room now."

The Earl of Ornum cleared his throat, and said in a low rumble, "'Fraid you're probably right, Gertrude."

Laura Cremond said spitefully, "What about you, Gertrude? You've got more to lose than any of us, haven't you?"

10

Monday morning dawned with its customary inevitability.

With it came the news that there had been a road traffic accident at Tappett's Corner on the main Berebury to Luston Road the night before. Superintendent Leeyes was not pleased about this.

"A ruddy great pileup," he moaned, flinging down the report in front of Inspector Sloan as soon as he arrived on duty. "One woman driver who wouldn't have been safe out with a pram, one commercial vehicle with no business to be on the road at all on a Sunday ..."

Inspector Sloan picked up the paper and began to read.

"And a family saloon," said Leeyes, "driven by two old women."

The report said that it had been driven by a husband with his wife sitting beside him, but Sloan knew what the superintendent meant. He had been speaking figuratively. There were some real figures, too.

Two people had been taken to hospital and three vehicles to the suspect garage.

"If there's anybody in my division getting a kickback out of this, Sloan," threatened Leeyes, "there's going to be real trouble."

"Yes, sir." He looked at the report. "It is the nearest garage to Tappett's Corner."

"I know that."

"And they're the only people with heavy lifting gear for this van."

"I know that, too, and it doesn't help, does it?"

"No, sir."

It didn't.

If there was something wrong there was something wrong and explanations were neither here nor there.

"This other business, Sloan ..." Only a true policeman, jealous in honor, would have such an order of priority. "How far have you got? We can't hang on to a case like this, you know."

"Some of the way, sir." Sloan knew Superintendent Leeyes wouldn't want anyone else here while he was worried about Inspector Harpe's men. "I think the deceased was killed in the library between four o'clock and half-past five on Friday afternoon."

Leeyes grunted.

"He was last seen alive," went on Sloan, "by Lady Eleanor, the Earl's daughter, just before four and by the butler, Dillow, immediately after that."

"But by five-thirty …"

"By five-thirty. That was when the vicar, Mr. Walter Ames, arrived at Ornum House in response to a message—"

"A message?"

"A message to the effect that his friend, Mr. Meredith, had made an important discovery—"

"What!"

"I'm afraid so, sir."

"What sort of discovery?"

"We don't know, sir. Yet. All we know is that he telephoned the vicar's house during that afternoon and left a message with the vicar's wife asking Mr. Ames to step around to the house as soon as he could." Sloan paused. "I think that by the time he got there Mr. Meredith was dead."

"Someone else knew about his discovery?"

"Yes, sir. I think so." He coughed. "The telephone at Ornum House is somewhat public, sir. It's in the entrance hall. Anyone could have heard him."

"Someone did?"

"I'm very much afraid so, sir."

Leeyes grunted again. "Go on."

"There are bloodstains at the far end of the last bay in the library. I'm having them analyzed this morning. He could well have been killed there and left there until the opportunity arose to take his body to the armory."

"Without being seen?"

"It was a chance that would have to be taken. I should not imagine that the library was used all that often and the bloodstains are at the far end of the last bay. In fact Mr. Ames did look in the library for the deceased and called out his name—but when he did not appear or answer he went away."

"Beyond call," observed Leeyes succinctly, "and recall."

"Exactly, sir. Then there are the muniments—"

"Documents," supplied Leeyes, "kept as evidence of rights or privilege."

"Thank you, sir. I thought they might be. Well, at some time after five-thirty on Friday afternoon when the vicar looked in the muniments room and noticed nothing amiss, and at some time before I got there myself yesterday afternoon, some person or persons unknown played havoc with them."

The superintendent's eyebrows shot up. "Ho ho!"

"Yes, sir. All we know at present about who did it was that they were wearing a size six and a half lady's shoe."

"A woman, eh?"

"Someone wearing a lady's shoe," said Sloan more precisely. "There are three ladies in the house who take that size in footwear. Mrs. Laura Cremond, Miss Gertrude Cremond, and the housekeeper, Mrs. Morley." He paused. "It's a popular size."

The superintendent stroked his chin. "So there was something that mattered in the muniments room."

"Something they thought mattered," Sloan corrected him obliquely.

"Motive?"

"Perhaps, sir," said Sloan, and told him about the threatened earldom.

"Ah, Sloan, kind hearts may be more than coronets, but when it comes to the church ..."

"Quite so, sir. If it ... er ... should turn out to be that sort of crunch then there are a fair number of people with a vested interest in the status quo, I agree, but ..."

"But what?"

"That particular discovery was relatively old hat by last Friday."

"How relatively?"

"The immediate family and the steward had known all about it for nearly a week."

"Stewards," interrupted the superintendent didactically, "are notoriously untrustworthy."

"Unjust," murmured Sloan, whose Sunday schooling had been impeccable. "I don't know if this one is or not yet. Anyway, if the Ornums and their steward had known about it for so long, what I don't quite see is why the deceased should suddenly get excited on Friday afternoon. If it's the same discovery, that is."

"How soon did the nephews get to hear about it?" The superintendent's own theory of relativity was more simply stated than Einstein's.

The nearer the degree of relationship, the greater the likelihood of murder.

"Miles Cremond and his wife were told when they arrived on Thursday for the weekend."

"The weekend?" echoed Leeyes. "Thursday?" Police weekends began at noon on Saturdays.

"Yes, sir. He works in London."

"That explains it. What at?"

"For a shipping company," said Sloan carefully, "as a figurehead, I should imagine."

"No head for figures though?"

"I shouldn't think he would go much beyond a batting average, sir. He's with the Pedes Line."

"They're in deep water," said Leeyes, unconsciously apposite. "Everyone knows that."

"Yes, sir."

"And the other nephew? The artist one."

"I don't know when he found out, sir." Sloan paused. "He's a bit of a puzzle."

"I'm tired of crazy mixed-up kids, Sloan."

"I don't quite know what to make of him, sir," he said seriously. "I think he could well be one of those. I've put in some enquiries about both nephews to London."

"Good. The deceased's sister," went on Leeyes. "Has she turned up yet?"

Sloan shook his head. "There's no sign of her. The postmistress thinks she's visiting a friend, but doesn't know for sure. Crosby's been round the outside of the house to make certain she's not hanging in the woodshed or anything like that, but I hardly like to ask for a warrant to break in for a better look."

Superintendent Leeyes' grunt indicated that he wouldn't get one if he asked.

"What now, Sloan? I can't keep headquarters out of the case forever."

"I'm just waiting for the post-mortem report on the deceased from Dr. Dabbe, and then I'm going back to Ornum House."

"Gadzooks," observed the superintendent sardonically, "strapping his vitals, is he?"

Detective Constable Crosby was in Sloan's office struggling with the small print in the *Peerage*. "A telephone message from London, sir. Just come through."

"The nephews?"

Crosby shook his head. "Firm of solicitors, name of Oaten. Oaten and Cossington—representing the Earl of Ornum. The senior partner is on his way down now."

Sloan was not surprised. He pointed to the book. "Have you got the succession sorted out?"

"Yes, sir. Sir, did you know that once everyone was either an earl or a churl?" Crosby had obviously begun at the very beginning. "They were all divided into those two groups."

"People have always been divided into two groups, Constable, and the sooner you get that into your head the better." At school he had learned about patricians and plebeians, as a young man about proletarians and … proletarians and … Sloan couldn't think now who the others had been, but he could still remember getting very excited about it at the time. It had seemed so important. Now that he was older he knew the grouping was simpler than that.

Oneself versus The Rest.

"And," went on Crosby industriously, "they made men earls when they didn't want to make them marquesses or dukes."

"You don't say," remarked Sloan. "Status rearing its ugly head again."

"Beg pardon, sir?"

"Nothing. The Ornums …"

"Yes, sir. It's all down here." He paused. "Everything."

"Everything?"

"Well, sir, they don't half say what they mean."

Sloan regarded the heavy tome with respect. That wasn't always the case with big books. "Good."

"Very clear," said Crosby primly.

"Oh?"

The constable squinted down at the page and read aloud, " 'The succession is limited to heirs of the body male,' sir, that's what it says here."

"Indeed," said Sloan gravely.

"And something about Lords of Creation."

"Are you sure?"

Crosby took another look. "Lords of the First Creation."

"Ornum isn't one of those, surely?" Not with a Norman keep and a Tudor great hall.

"No, sir, I don't think so. Henry the Eighth gave them extra land after some battle or other …"

"England, home, and booty," murmured Sloan.

"And they seem to have been hereditary beacon keepers to the Crown for the County of Calleshire since the reign of Queen Elizabeth the First."

"Very useful thing to know," agreed Sloan, "but what about now?"

"Lord Henry inherits."

"And if anything happens to Lord Henry?"

"The Honorable Miles Cremond, eldest son of the younger brother of the twelfth Earl, is next in succession."

"I thought he might be," said Sloan.

"I can't find Miss Gertrude Cremond anywhere …"

"Too far from the main line."

"But the two old ladies are here. Daughters of the eleventh Earl."

"That's going back a bit."

"And I've found William Murton. At least"—Crosby put a large fore-finger on a tiny line of print—"I think so. It says here after Lady Eliza-beth ... 'married W. Murton of Ornum, one s.' "

"That," said Sloan solemnly, "is what happens when you run away with your groom. We will make a point of seeing William Murton again very soon. Now, this business of the Earl not being the Earl ..."

Crosby slapped the book. "Not here. . . . There's just a bit about their escutcheon ..."

"No blot?" Deadpan.

"Not yet, sir." Crosby grinned. "There's quite a long piece about their coat of arms, but I didn't think you'd want to go into that."

"You never can tell," said Sloan. "The Bordens had a lion, rampant, on their crest, bearing a battleaxe, proper. Let me have a look."

Whatever doubts existed about the title to the Earldom of Ornum there would be none about the parentage of Lord Henry Cremond.

Seen together, the Earl and his son were absurdly alike. Seen sitting between his father and mother, Lord Henry would have done for an illus-tration for one of Mr. Mendel's textbooks on hereditary characteristics. He had her skin, his coloring, the Cremond nose, her vague manner, his mannerisms.

Lady Eleanor, their daughter, who was there too, was less certainly a Cremond in appearance. More definite than her mother, less pessimistic than her father, more practical than either, she had been leavened by a vein of common sense in sheer reaction to a mother as distrait as hers.

The four of them were in the sitting-room of the private apartments. They looked like a *tableau vivant* of a family.

Until the Earl spoke.

"I don't like it," he said. "It's not like William not to be short of money."

"No," agreed Lord Henry.

"Always has been."

"Yes."

"Should have thought he always would be."

"Yes."

"After all, there's no reason for him to change." The Earl pulled his mustache and corrected himself. "There's no reason that we know of for him to change."

"No."

"His father was the same. Never a bean."

Henry nodded.

"My father," went on the Earl gloomily, "had to support his father or else see m'sister starve. Couldn't do that."

"No."

"And you, my boy, will probably have to support his children."

"Yes."

"Can't let them starve either. Not family."

"'Course not," murmured Lord Henry.

"But William isn't married yet, dear," said the Countess.

"He should be," retorted her husband cryptically.

The Countess looked blank.

"More than once," added her husband.

"Harry, what do you mean?"

"A roving eye," said the Earl warmly, "that's what that young man's got. And no money to go with it."

"But he hasn't got any children, dear, surely."

"Their mothers say he has."

"No!"

"I understand," said the Earl drily, "that there have been several unsuccessful attempts to get him as far as the altar."

"You mean …" A wave of comprehension swept over Millicent Ornum's face.

"I do. Paternity and maintenance."

"Well, really, Harry, I do think that's the …"

"Mother, there's no use making a fuss now," Eleanor interrupted her realistically. "After all, it comes from our side of the family."

"Eleanor!"

"Well, it does. Aunt Elizabeth wasn't known as Bad Betty for nothing."

This was too much for the Countess. She appealed to her husband.

"Harry, I don't need to remind you that your father would never have her name mentioned in this house as long as he lived."

"True, my dear, very true." The Earl's hand sought solace by his mustache. "Perhaps he was wiser than we knew. It does seem to lead to trouble. Shall I apply a similar interdiction?"

But by then his wife had caught up with an earlier imputation.

"Eleanor."

"Yes, Mother?"

"William's mother was not on our side of the family."

"She was …"

"She was on your father's side, which is different."

This being true of all families, noble and otherwise, Eleanor did not debate it. "Yes, Mother," she said obediently.

"I must say it's not like William not to be on his beam ends by the time he comes down to Ornum," Lord Henry changed the subject with the deftness of long experience.

"I don't like it," reiterated the Earl. "I don't like it at all."

Lord Henry, who lacked a mustache to tug, instead fondled the tassel of the chair cushion. "Laura and Gertrude don't exactly hit it off, do they?"

"Never have," said his father. "Difficult woman, Gertrude."

"Laura's no peacemaker either," said Eleanor.

"Rather not," agreed Henry. He cleared his throat. "She and Miles were late for dinner on Friday."

"I noticed," said the Earl heavily.

"And she went to bed uncommonly early."

"I know." A permanent air of melancholy seemed to have settled on the Earl of Ornum.

"They're staying on—Miles and Laura, I mean," said the Countess, "because of this business about poor Mr. Meredith, and Dillow's not having his day off today because of all the reporters coming."

There was a moment's gloomy silence, and then:

"There's something else, isn't there?" said Lady Eleanor.

Her brother looked up. "What's that?"

"Something that no one seems to have thought about," said Lady Eleanor. "We all think poor Ossy was murdered because he knew something."

"Yes …"

"What we don't know is why someone went to all that trouble to put him in the armor."

"To stop him being found," said Lord Henry promptly. "His sister is away. He isn't going to be really missed for ages."

"Exactly." Eleanor waved a hand. "That's what I mean. He might not have been found for days."

"So?"

"So the delay was important. That's right, Father, isn't it?"

The Earl sighed. "I'm afraid so, my dear."

"Why?" asked Lord Henry immediately.

"I don't know."

Every now and then Millicent Ornum came into the conversation with a remark that proved she had been listening.

She did so now.

"I expect," she said brightly, "it's because of something that hasn't happened yet."

11

Inspector Sloan telephoned Charles Purvis, the steward, at Ornum as soon as he could.

"You'll be having some visitors at the house today," he said.

"If you mean the press," responded Purvis promptly, "they're here now."

Sloan hadn't meant the press. "No, the vicar. I want him to be there when we open up the armory again, and some people from our forensic laboratory. They'll want to examine the library and the muniments room and so on ..."

"Very well, Inspector. I'll see that they are allowed in."

"And the county archivist."

"Ah ..."

"With the Earl's permission, that is. We've asked him to come over from the county record office at Calleford to examine the muniments for us."

"He'll come all right," said Charles Purvis cheerfully. "Like a shot."

"Oh?"

"He's been trying to get a really good look at them for years, only Meredith would never let him."

"Really?" Sloan tucked that fact away in his mind, too. "And I would like to see the four regular guides to the house, please. The ones who took people round this weekend."

Purvis promised to arrange this with them straightaway. "About eleven o'clock suit you for that, then, Inspector?"

Sloan said that would do very nicely and rang off.

Then for the second time P.C. Crosby drove him out to Ornum. On this occasion they stopped first in the village itself.

Cremond Cottages was a neat little row of four dwellings, with the initials H.C. carved into a small tablet in the middle over the date 1822. Though it was by no means early by the time they knocked on the door of number four, William Murton had not yet shaved.

"Ah, gentlemen, good morning, and welcome to my humble home." There was the faintest of ironic stresses on the word "humble." He ushered them in. "I thought you'd be along sooner or later."

The downstairs rooms of the cottage had been knocked together into one and decorated in a manner more redolent of town than country. There was a painting hanging over the fireplace that Sloan took to be an abstract. There was a large eye in one corner of it; the rest was an unidentifiable mixture of color and design.

Constable Crosby saw the picture as he entered the room and took a deep breath.

Sloan said swiftly, "Is that your own work, Mr. Murton?"

The artist nodded. "My grandmother—my paternal grandmother, needless to say, was fond of texts on walls. She had this one hanging over her bed."

"This one?"—faintly.

"Well, the same thing in words. I prefer to express the idea in paint, that's all."

"I see," said Sloan cautiously. He took a second look at the painting.

"You've recognized it, of course," said Murton ironically.

Sloan, who only knew what he didn't like in modern art, said, "I don't know that I have, sir."

"Thou God Seest Me." There was no mistaking the mocking tone now. "Reaction against all that traditional stuff up at the house, you know."

"Quite so." If the painting was anything to go by, it was a pretty violent reaction.

"And over there …" Murton pointed to where an excessively modern wall bracket in the shape of a nude female figure—just this side of actionable—supported a light fitting.

Constable Crosby's eyes bulged and his lips started to move.

"Over there," continued Murton, "my grandmother had 'There's No Place Like Home' worked in embroidery."

"Did she?"

"Set tastefully in a ring of roses."

Inspector Sloan, whose who hobby was growing roses—rather than growing girls—said, "That must have been very nice, sir."

"Pure Victoriana, of course."

"Naturally, sir." He coughed. "This *is* your home, I take it?"

"Well, now, Inspector, that's a good question." William Murton's eyes danced mischievously. "It's like this. By virtue of long residence I'm a protected tenant here …"

That, decided Sloan privately, must have caused a certain amount of chagrin in some quarters.

"So," went on Murton, "it would be downright foolish of me to leave, wouldn't it?"

"I see what you mean, sir."

"So I stay. After all"—gravely—"my family have lived here a very long time."

"Quite so."

"And there's nothing wrong with being a cottager, you know. My father was a cottager."

"So," said Sloan impassively, "you use this for a weekend cottage."

"Got it in one, Inspector."

"You come down every weekend?"

"Not quite"—tantalizingly—"every weekend. Just ... er ... every now and then."

"Why this particular one?"

Murton shrugged a pair of surprisingly broad shoulders. "The spirit moved me. I didn't come down to do poor Ossy in, if that's what you mean."

"You knew him, of course?"

"Oh yes. We were all brought up together as children, you know. Like puppies. Miles' parents were abroad a lot and mine couldn't provide for me properly"—he grimaced—"so ..."

"So," concluded Sloan for him, "you had the worst of both worlds."

Murton looked at him curiously. "That's right, Inspector. I was brought up half a gentleman. You think as children that the world's an equal place. It's later when you realize that Henry gets the lot."

"Disturbing," agreed Sloan.

"Especially when you're older than he is and you can see his father had the lot, too. And all your father had was this."

"Quite so, sir."

"That's what's made me into a sponger."

"A sponger?"

"A sponger, Inspector, that's what I said. I don't earn my keep like Cousin Gertrude cleaning chandeliers for dear life and I don't stay on the fringes like Laura, hoping for pickings."

"I see, sir."

"And I don't stand around praying for miracles like that efficient ass Charles Purvis. I'm a plain hanger-on."

"I see, sir. And for the rest of the time you do what?"

"This and that," he said easily.

Sloan could find the proper answer by picking up the telephone. He said instead, "Now, as to Friday ..."

William Murton hadn't a great deal to tell him about Friday.

Yes, he had originally intended to come only for the weekend.

Yes, he had come down on Friday afternoon.

By train.

About half-past five.

He had spent Friday evening at the cottage.

Alone.

Saturday he had stayed in bed until teatime and the evening he had spent in The Ornum Arms.

At least twenty people would confirm this, including Ebeneezer Lambert down the road.

If the inspector should by any remote chance happen to see old Lambert he might tell him that he had lost his bet and owed him, William Murton, Esquire, a fiver.

And not to forget the esquire. We might not all be earls, but there was no law yet against us all being esquires, was there?

And if the inspector wanted to know who he thought had done it …

The great-aunts.

"In fact, sir," said Crosby, as he drove Inspector Sloan from the cottage up to the house, "we aren't short of suspects, are we?"

"No."

"That chap ran right through the lot for us. Did you notice, sir?"

"He didn't mention Dillow," said Sloan, "and he didn't mention Mr. Ames."

"The vicar?" said Crosby. "I hadn't thought of him."

"You should think of everyone, Constable. That's what you're here for."

"Yes, sir."

"He came to the house at about the right time on Friday afternoon," said Sloan. "He told us so."

"Yes, sir."

"And he knows about armor."

"He doesn't look like a murderer."

"Neither did Crippen."

This profound observation kept Constable Crosby quiet until they reached Ornum House.

Dillow was at hand as ever.

"The vicar is in the great hall, gentlemen, waiting your arrival. Mr. Purvis is in the morning room interviewing the press …"

"The Queen is in the parlor eating bread and honey," muttered the incorrigible Crosby, irritated by all this formality.

"Very good, sir," murmured the butler smoothly, not at all put out.

Sloan reflected that an irrepressible police constable must be child's play to a man who had worked for that eccentric millionaire Baggles.

"And, sir, Edith, the housemaid—you indicated you wished to speak to her—is available whenever you wish."

"Now," suggested Sloan. "I just wanted to know when she last went into the library."

Dillow produced Edith immediately. She was willing and cheerful, but not bright.

"Yeth, sir"—she was slightly adenoidal too—"Saturday morning, sir. There was nobody there then."

This was clarified by Sloan into *no body*.

"That's right," agreed Edith. "Nobody at all."

"Did you go right into the library—to the very far end?"

"Oh, yeth, sir."

"Passed the farthest bay?"

"Yeth, sir. Because of the General."

"The General?"

"Yeth, sir. He gets very dusty if you leave him over the day."

"Ah, you mean the bust ..."

Edith looked as if she hadn't liked to mention the word in front of three gentlemen. She nodded.

"And what time would that have been?"

"Nine o'clock, sir. After I cleared the breakfasts."

"Thank you, Edith. That's all."

Edith looked relieved and went. In the distance at the top of the great balustraded staircase they caught a glimpse of Cousin Gertrude tramping across the upper landing.

Mr. Ames was waiting for them in the great hall. He looked older in broad daylight.

"We've just been checking a few facts," said Sloan truthfully. "The family and so forth."

"One of the oldest in the county," said the vicar. "Hereditary beacon keepers to the Crown for Calleshire since the reign of Queen Elizabeth the First ..."

Sloan hadn't meant that sort of fact.

"She was afraid of the Spanish coming, you know, Inspector."

"Really?"

"The old Norman tower above the keep has a flat roof." The vicar smiled a clerical smile. "The Norman invasion, you remember, had been a successful one. A highly successful one."

"Yes, sir"—stolidly.

"A beacon fire lit there could be seen from the roof of Calle Castle, which is some way inland. They in turn would light a beacon fire there and so on."

"I see, sir, thank you."

"And then there was Charles the Second."

Sloan was not interested in Charles the Second.

"He," said Mr. Ames, "was afraid of the Dutch. Now George the Third …"

Sloan had come about murder not history.

"He was worried about the French. Napoleon, you know."

"I don't think the historical side concerns us, Vicar." It was, after all, as Superintendent Leeyes had said, the twentieth century.

"And then," said Mr. Ames, unheeding, "there was 1940 and the Germans. We had a really big beacon all ready for firing then. Bert Hackle's father—old Hackle—he used to keep lookout …"

"Quite so, sir. Now if we might come back to the more immediate past— like Friday."

With police-like patience he set about taking the vicar through all the details of his abortive visit to the house following Osborne Meredith's message. Mr. Ames obediently detailed his story for the second time.

He had had a message, he had come up to the house, he had not seen Meredith in the muniments room or anywhere else.

"The documents chests," said Sloan suddenly. "Were they shut or open?"

The vicar screwed up his eyes the better to remember. "Open," he said eventually. "That's what made me think Meredith would still be about somewhere."

"Did you see anyone else while you were here?"

"Dillow—he said he thought Meredith had gone home as he wasn't about—and Miss Cremond—Miss Gertrude Cremond, you know. She was cleaning the chandelier in here."

They all looked upwards.

"A very lovely piece," said Mr. Ames. "French crystal."

"Was she alone?" asked Sloan.

The vicar nodded. "Miss Cremond," he murmured diplomatically, "is in total charge of all the Ornum china and glass. Lady Eleanor helps her with the flowers, but Miss Cremond handles all the rest herself."

"I see, sir."

"It was all still down on the table when I saw her," said Mr. Ames. "Hundreds of pieces."

"A day's work," agreed Sloan, turning to go.

As he did so he stopped in his tracks.

Sloan would not have described himself as a sensitive man. If he thought of himself at all it was as an ordinary policeman—warts and all. But at that moment—as he stood with Crosby and the vicar in the great hall—the atavistic sensation came to him that they were being watched.

It was a very primitive feeling.

The hairs on the back of his neck erected themselves and an involuntary little shiver passed down his spine. Primeval reactions that were established long before man built himself his first shelter—let alone medieval castles.

Sloan let his gaze run casually round the great hall. It was not long before he spotted the peephole up near the roof in the dim corner behind and beyond the minstrels' gallery. He drifted slowly towards the door under the gallery and so out of sight of the peephole.

Once there, he changed to a swift run, going up the vast staircase as quickly as he could, his sense of direction working full blast.

He kept right at the top of the stair and chose the farthest door. He flung it open on a small, paneled room.

There was nobody there.

But in the opposite wall, low down, was a little window giving not to the out-of-doors but to another room. He stepped across and peered through it.

He was looking down at the great hall. From where he stood he could see the vicar still talking to Crosby. The constable was standing listening in an attitude of patient resignation. Sloan straightened up again and stepped back into the corridor.

And somewhere not very far away he heard a door closing gently.

12

Charles Purvis was being put through his paces by the press and he was not enjoying it.

For one thing, though, he was deeply thankful. With the help of Dillow he had at least managed to bottle up all the reporters in the same room. The thought of a stray one happening upon Lady Alice was too terrible to contemplate.

"Gentlemen," he began, "I can give you very little information—"

"Can we see the Earl?" asked one of them immediately, mentioning a newspaper that Purvis had only seen wrapped round fish.

"The Earl is not at home."

"You mean he isn't here?"

"No," said Purvis, "just not at home."

"You mean he won't see us?"

"His Lordship is not available," insisted Charles Purvis. He had a fleeting vision of a subheading "No Comment from Earl of Ornum." (What the reporters wrote, in fact, was, "Earl Silent.")

"Do we understand, Steward, that the body was in the armor all day on Saturday and Sunday while visitors were being shown round?"

"I believe so," said Purvis unhappily as the reporters scribbled away. ("Little did those who paid their half crowns at the weekend know that …")

"How do you spell 'archivist'?" said somebody.

The man from the oldest established newspaper told him.

"When are you open again?" asked another man.

"Wednesday," said Purvis cautiously, "I think."

"That your usual day?"

"Yes." (They wrote, " 'Business as Usual,' Says Steward.")

"That means you won't actually have closed at all?"

"Yes." (" 'We Never Close,' Says Earl's Steward.")

"I reckon this is the first stately home murder, boys."

Purvis winced and the others nodded.

"This Earl of yours …" The voice came from a man at the back.

"Yes?"

"He's not much of a talker, is he?"

"A talker?" Charles Purvis was discovering the hard way that stone-walling is an underrated art—not only on the cricket pitch but every-where else, too.

"That's right," said the reporter, who had been doing his homework. "He's been a member of the House of Lords for thirty years."

"Yes?"

"I've looked him up."

"Oh?"

"He's only spoken twice. On red deer."

"That's right."

"Both times."

"It's his subject."

There were hoots of merry laughter at this.

Purvis flushed. "He has his own herd, you know, and ..."

But the reporters were already on to their next questions.

"Our art man," said a crime reporter, "our Old Art man, this is, tells me you've got a Holbein here."

"That's right," confirmed Purvis.

"What's the Earl doing taking in washing when he's got a Holbein?"

Purvis hadn't expected the interview to go like this. "It's of a member of the family," he retorted, stung. "That's why."

("Steward says Holbein would have been sold long ago but for senti-mental reasons," they wrote.)

"Our new art man," said another newspaperman, "says the Earl's nephew has just had an exhibition. Murton's the name. William Murton."

"Oh?" This was news to Charles Purvis. "I didn't know that."

"One of the smaller galleries," said the man, "but quite well written up."

"The other nephew," a bald man informed them gratuitously, "Miles Cremond, is with the Pedes Shipping line."

"Is he now?"

"And our city editor," he went on, "says they're pretty ropey these days."

"Now is the time for all share-holding rats to leave the sinking ship?" suggested an amiably cynical man near the door.

"Pretty well," admitted the bald chap.

"Has he got any other good tips, Curly?"

"Buy the rag and see," suggested the bald man. "Money well spent, they tell me."

They were surprisingly well-informed.

They had already sucked the reference books dry. They had taken in a visit to a gratified Mrs. Pearl Fisher at Paradise Row, Luston, on their way to Ornum. (The whole street had ordered copies of tomorrow's papers.) They had attempted to suborn Edith, the housemaid, at the back door of Ornum House before coming round to the front, and they had got nowhere at all with Superintendent Leeyes—and all before breakfast, so to speak.

"The family," said a man with a disillusioned face, whose paper specialized in what it was pleased to call "human interest." "Can we have some pictures?"

"No," said Purvis.

"They've got a son and a daughter, haven't they?"

"Yes"—tightly.

"Some pictures would be nice. Family group and so forth."

"No."

"I think we've got one of Lady Eleanor on the files anyway."

Purvis blanched.

"Some charity performance somewhere."

Charles Purvis breathed again.

"She's not engaged?" suggested the reporter hopefully.

"No."

"Nor opened a boutique or an antique shop or anything like that?"

"No."

"No family secrets passed down from father to son on his twenty-first birthday?"

"No."

"No secret rooms?"

"I'm afraid not." Purvis was genuinely regretful. If there had been a secret room in Ornum House he would willingly have taken them to see it. Anything to divert their questioning.

"Sure?"

"The tax-rating people would have found it," said the steward bitterly.

"The victim's sister," said a young man with long hair and a red tie. "What's happened to her?"

Purvis relaxed a little. "We don't know. We think she's visiting friends, but we don't know where." He looked round the assembled company. "That's really where we could do with your cooperation, gentlemen. She probably doesn't know about this terrible business ..." Out of the corner of his eye he saw the "human interest" man writing rapidly, "... and the police hope that she will read about the death and get in touch with them."

"Will do."

Charles Purvis doubted very much if Miss Meredith ever read either the "human interest" paper or the one with which the young man with the long hair and the red tie was associated, but sooner or later she would hear.

To Purvis' distress the newspaper of which his Lordship had been a loyal reader all his life had also sent a reporter. He, too, had a question.... It was like treachery.

"The weapon, Mr. Purvis, can you tell us what it was?"

He shook his head. "I understand the weapon has not yet been found."

He was wrong.

The weapon had been found.

On the upstairs landing Inspector Sloan had met up with the team from the forensic laboratory, a taciturn pair of men who knew a bloodstain when they saw one. They had seen one on the spine of a book in the library and now they were looking at another.

They were all in the armory. One suit of armor had gone—*the* suit of armor—and the gap stood out like a missing tooth. The armory itself looked like a gigantic game of chess after a good opening move.

Detective Constable Crosby had began by working from quite a different premise—that one of the hundred and seventy weapons listed in the catalogue would be missing. So he and Mr. Ames had been conducting a bizarre roll-call.

"One anelace."

"Present."

"One voulge."

"Yes. A very early piece," said the vicar with satisfaction. "Not many of them about."

"A tschinke?"

"That's right. The tenth Earl brought that back with him from abroad. It's a sort of sporting gun."

Crosby eyed it warily. If that was the sort of souvenir that came from foreign parts he would stay at home.

"He was an ambassador," said the vicar.

"I know." Crosby moved his finger down the list and said cautiously, "A pair of dolphins."

"Both here. Lifting tackle, you know, for guns."

Crosby didn't know. "Three bastard swords," he continued.

"All here."

At the third attempt, "A guardapolvo."

"Yes."

"A Lucerne hammer."

"Yes."

Crosby hesitated. "A spontoon."

"Yes."

"A brandistock." Crosby looked up from the list. "What's that?"

"A weapon with a tubular shaft concealing a blade ..."

Crosby lost interest.

The vicar pointed. "You can jerk the blade forward."

"We call it a flick knife," said Crosby laconically. "Next. A godentag. What's that?"

"A club thickening towards the head," said Mr. Ames, indicating it with his hand, "and topped with an iron spike. Hullo, it's not hanging quite straight—someone must have—"

"Don't touch it," shouted Crosby, dropping the list and making for the wall.

Mr. Ames' hands fell back to his side, but he went on looking.

So did the pair from the forensic laboratory—only they looked through a powerful pocket lens and they looked long and hard.

"Blood," said the senior of the two, "and a couple of hairs."

Inspector Sloan turned to the vicar. "What did you say it was called, sir?"

"A godentag," said Mr. Ames. "Taken literally it means 'Good Morning.'"

Detective Constable Crosby caught the affirmative nod from the laboratory technician to Inspector Sloan and interpreted it correctly. "If that's what did it, sir, shouldn't it be 'Good Night'?"

Charles Purvis had been as good as his word. He came down to the armory to tell Sloan that the four guides were waiting for him in the oriel room.

"They're all there except Hackle and he's working in the knot garden if you want to see him, too."

Inspector Sloan hesitated. A knot garden sounded like a Noh play. "Where's that?" he asked cautiously.

"Just this side of the belvedere," said the steward, trying to be helpful. "By the gazebo."

"And the oriel room?" said Sloan, giving up. It was like learning a new language.

"I'll take you there," said Purvis. He hadn't finished with the press—he didn't suppose you ever finished with the press—but he had done what he could.

The oriel room had been a felicitous choice on the part of Purvis. It was a room that was never shown to the public, while still not being quite the same as the private apartments. Mrs. Mompson, Miss Cleepe, Mrs. Nutting, and Mr. Feathers were there and Dillow was plying them with coffee.

Pseudo-privilege for pseudo-guests.

The thin Miss Cleepe declined sugar, the tubby Mrs. Nutting took two spoonfuls.

"I know I shouldn't," she said, "but I do like it."

As usual, Mrs. Mompson remained a trifle aloof. "Poor little Miss Meredith," she said with condescension. Mrs. Mompson called other women "little" irrespective of their size. "I do feel so sorry for her."

"I feel more sorry for Meredith myself," said Mr. Feathers practically. "Not the sort of end I'd fancy."

Mrs. Nutting shivered. "Nor me. We must help the inspector all we can."

It wasn't very much.

Sloan took them through the previous Saturday and Sunday—not so many people on the Saturday, but then there never are—but Sunday was crowded. They wouldn't be surprised if Sunday had been a record. (It wouldn't stay that way for long if it had been, thought Sloan. Not after tomorrow's papers came out.)

Mr. Feathers had noticed nothing out of the ordinary in the great hall. Miss Gertrude Cremond had been along to see the chandelier in daylight, and expressed herself pleased with it. It wouldn't need doing again for the season, otherwise all had been as usual.

Mrs. Nutting reported one small child had got under the fourposter while her back was turned, but had been extricated (and spanked) without difficulty.

"Otherwise," she said cheerfully, "just as usual. Same sort of people. Same questions."

Miss Cleepe, as angular as Mrs. Nutting was curved, twisted her hands together. The long gallery had been much the same. The usual difficulty of parties made up of people who really cared about painting and those who neither knew nor cared.

"It's so trying if you sense that they're bored," she said, "but the Holbein always interests them."

"After you've told them what it's worth," said Mr. Feathers brutally.

She sighed. "That's so. They always take a second look then." She put down her coffee cup. "And of course they always ask about the ghost. Always."

Mrs. Mompson, who had for some time been trying to engineer an exchange of pictures between the long gallery and the drawing room, said, "That picture doesn't get the light it should in the long gallery."

"It is rather dark," agreed Miss Cleepe. "It's such a low narrow room, and the bulb in its own little light was broken. Dillow's getting another for me."

"I've always said that over the fireplace in the drawing room is where that picture should be," declared Mrs. Mompson. "Where everyone could really see it properly."

"I don't know about that I'm sure," said Miss Cleepe nervously. "After all, too much light might be bad for the picture."

"It's practically in the half dark in the long gallery where it is. Halfway from each window and not very good windows at that." Mrs. Mompson had over the fireplace in the drawing room at present an eighteenth-century portrayal of the goddess of plenty, Ceres, that she had long wanted to be rid of. The goddess had been depicted somewhat fulsomely and Mrs. Mompson did not think the artist's conception of that bountiful creature quite nice.

"I think," she went on, "the Holbein would be seen to real advantage over my fireplace."

Miss Cleepe flushed. To lose from her showing ground the most valuable item in the house and the ghost at one fell swoop was more than she could bear.

"Oh, dear!" she fluttered. "Do you really? I should be very sorry to lose the Judge. Very sorry. I always feel he's a real interest to those to whom the other pictures mean nothing."

Inspector Sloan made no move to stop them talking. The policeman's art was to listen and to watch. Not to do. At least not when witnesses were talking to each other, almost oblivious of an alien presence in their midst. Almost but not quite.

Mrs. Mompson, who had no wish for an immediate ruling on the subject of the Holbein from Charles Purvis, said firmly, "Nothing, I assure you, Inspector, out of the ordinary happened in the drawing room while I was in charge."

Sloan, who would have been surprised if it had, nodded.

"One young woman went so far as to finger the epergne," she went on imperiously. "But I soon put a stop to that."

"Quite so, madam. Thank you all very …"

Miss Cleepe had not done.

In a voice that trembled slightly she said, "I really don't think I could possibly manage the long gallery without the Holbein."

Sloan was ringing back to base. Base wasn't very pleased at his news.

"Someone," declared Sloan, "has tried to get into the muniments room since we sealed it up yesterday."

"They have, have they? What for?"

"I don't know, sir. I'd arranged for the county archivist to come over and start going through the records. When Crosby went up there with him he found someone had had a go at the lock."

"There's something in there," said Leeyes.

"Yes, sir."

"And someone's still after it."

"Yes, sir. They haven't got it though. The locks held."

"Just as well," grunted Leeyes. "By the way, Sloan, I've just had the Ornums' lawyer here. He's on his way out to you now. Watch him."

"Yes, sir."

"One of those clever chaps," said Leeyes resentfully. "Said he was representing the Earl's interests. Representing them!" Leeyes snorted. "Guarding them like a hawk, I'd say."

Sloan was not surprised. People like the Ornums went straight to the top and got the very best. He said gloomily, "I suppose the Earl will be another of those who know the chief constable personally, too ..."

They were the bane of his existence, those sort of people, assuming that acquaintanceship was an absolution.

"Be your age, Sloan."

"I beg your pardon, sir?"

"The Earl wouldn't be bothered with people like the chief constable."

"Not be bothered with the chief constable?" echoed Sloan faintly.

"That's what I said. The Home Secretary, Sloan, was his fag at school, and the Attorney-General's his wife's third cousin, twice removed."

"Oh, dear."

"Exactly." Sloan heard the superintendent bring his hand down on his desk with a bang just as he did when he was standing in front of him. "So if there's any arresting to be done ..."

"Yes, sir." Sloan took the unspoken point and tried to check on something else. "The rules, sir, aren't they different for peers of the realm?"

"I don't know about the written ones, Sloan," said Leeyes ominously, "but the unwritten ones are."

"Yes, sir"—absently. He was thinking about the Tower of London. He and his wife, Margaret, had gone there on their honeymoon. Was it just a museum still or were there dark corners where extra special prisoners lay?

"You could call it a case," said Leeyes judicially, "where a wrongful arrest isn't going to help the career of the police officer making it."

"Quite so, sir." He cleared his throat. "I'm nowhere near that stage yet, sir, but we think we've found the murder weapon. A club called 'Good Morning.' "

"A club called 'Good Morning,' " said Leeyes heavily. "You wouldn't by any chance be trying to take the micky out of a police superintendent called Leeyes, would you, Sloan, because if you are ..."

"No, sir"—hastily. "It's number forty-nine in the catalogue and its other name is a godentag. The forensic boys have found blood and hair on it but no fingerprints. Dr. Dabbe hasn't seen it yet, of course, to confirm that ..."

"That reminds me," interrupted Leeyes. "Dr. Dabbe. He's been on the phone with his report."

"Oh?"

"These pathologists," grumbled the superintendent. "They upset everything."

"Why?"

"You said, Sloan, that the butler took Meredith his tea at four o'clock and collected the empty tray at five."

"That's right, sir. He saw him at four but not at five. And Lady Eleanor saw him just before teatime."

"Teatime, perhaps," said Leeyes, "but not tea."

"Not tea?"

"Nothing had passed deceased's lips for three hours before death. Dr. Dabbe says so. Killed on an empty stomach in fact."

"Somebody ate Meredith's tea," said Sloan, turning back the pages of his notebook.

"Very likely, but not Meredith," pointed out the superintendent with finality. "Dr. Dabbe says so."

13

"So somebody got him in between Dillow taking him his tea and him getting his teeth into it?" concluded Constable Crosby succinctly. He was still in the armory though the vicar and the laboratory people had gone.

"That's right." There were more elegant ways of putting it, but in essence Crosby was right. "Though after Meredith had made his celebrated discovery and telephoned the vicarage in Ornum."

"Do we know when that was, sir?"

"Mrs. Ames thinks it must have been about half-past three."

"Then we're getting nowhere fast," Crosby said, disappointed, slinging his notebook down on the table that Dillow had provided for them in a corner of the armory. (It was of inlaid walnut and quite unsuitable.)

"Oh?"

"William Murton was seen to get off the 5:27 P.M. Luston to Berebury slow train at Ornum Station on Friday afternoon and I still think he did it," said Crosby all in one breath.

Sloan regarded his constable with interest. "You do, do you? Why?"

"He's a painter for one thing."

"That's not a crime. Yet."

"What I mean, sir, is that he's a bit of an oddity."

"Nor is that."

"Suddenly he isn't short of money any more."

"Meredith wasn't a rich man," countered Sloan, "and the connection with this case and money is—to say the least—obscure." It would be there, of course—it nearly always was once you'd ruled out lust—but Sloan couldn't see where it lay.

"Yes, sir."

"Did you arrange for him to be watched?"

"Yes, sir. P.C. Bloggs is tailing him." He paused. "London came through on the blower."

"Well?"

Crosby sucked his lips. "From what they can make out he's in dead trouble with a woman."

The nearest Constable Crosby himself had ever come to being in trouble with a woman was being late off-duty, thus missing the start of the big picture.

There was something almost paternal in Sloan's tone. "If every man who was that, Crosby, committed a murder, we'd never get a rest day."

Crosby played his last card. "The Earl thinks he did it."

"I know. It's the best circumstantial evidence we've got that the Earl didn't do it himself. Not that William Murton didn't."

"The Earl?" echoed Crosby, shocked. "You don't think he did it, do you, sir?"

"No, as it happens, I don't, but he's a suspect like everyone else."

All people being equal, but some being more equal than others.

Especially earls.

It was a natural step from there to Lord Henry.

"That's another thing I've checked," said Crosby, "without any joy."

"What is?"

"His young Lordship's car. There is some blood down between the fan blade and the radiator. I've told those two vampire chaps—"

"Laboratory technicians"—mildly.

"Them. They're going to have a look when they've finished with the 'Good Morning.' "

"He could have put it there," pointed out Sloan.

"Yes, sir"—briefly. Crosby flicked back the pages of his notebook. "There are no fingerprints on the 'Good Morning' by the way."

"I hadn't expected there would be."

"And Mrs. Morley, the housekeeper, said she bandaged Lord Henry's hand for him after he cut it. Friday, it was. In the morning."

"I see."

"She saw the wound."

"Doubting Thomases," said Sloan bitterly, his mind darting back to his Sunday-school days. "That's what we should be called, isn't it? Not coppers."

"I couldn't say, I'm sure, sir," murmured Crosby. "Anyway, Mrs. Morley said it was quite a nasty cut. He couldn't have held a cricket bat."

"Or a godentag?"

"Not according to Mrs. Morley, he couldn't. She wanted him to have the doctor. Right across the palm, it was, and the index finger."

"And he got it from a motor car, not from squeezing a dead man into a metal suit of armor?"

Crosby's case rested on Mrs. Morley and he said so.

"I see," said Sloan. "So you think Lord Henry is out as a suspect, but William Murton still in?"

"Except that he got off the 5:27 all right," repeated Crosby, "because the station master saw him himself."

"And have you checked that he didn't nip up the line and get on at the station before?"

"Not yet," replied Crosby in a nicely shaded manner which implied he had been about to do so.

"I should," advised Sloan. "What size shoes does he take?"

Crosby stared. "I didn't notice, sir."

"I did. A nine, at least."

"He's a big chap," agreed Crosby cautiously.

"Too big for a lady's shoe, size six and a half, anyway," observed Sloan, turning back the pages of his own notebook. "And the Countess and Lady Eleanor both take a five."

"Handy, that."

"Handy?"

"They can share," said Crosby. "Like my sister does."

"Crosby, people like this do not share shoes."

"No, sir."

"Assuming"—severely—"that the person who left a heel mark in the muniments room did so inadvertently, and I think they did."

"Yes …"

"That means Miss Gertrude Cremond, Mrs. Laura Cremond, or Mrs. Morley went in there and turned everything upside down."

"Unless it was an outside job, sir."

"Crosby," Sloan controlled a sigh. "We both know this wasn't an outside job."

"Yes, sir."

"So one of the three went in there …"

"After Meredith was killed, sir, or before?"

"Well, he's hardly likely to have stood by and watched, is he now?"

"No, sir." Crosby scratched his forehead. "Miss Gertrude Cremond's big enough to have dotted a small man who was sitting down at the time, for all that she's not young."

"True."

"Mrs. Laura Cremond isn't."

"No. Neither was Lady Macbeth."

"Pardon, sir?"

"Lady Macbeth. Another small woman. She got someone killed."

"Secondhand, you mean, sir."

"Precisely."

"You think she might have egged on the Honorable Miles, sir?"

"Goaded would be a better word, Crosby."

"Yes, sir." He paused and said carefully, "I don't think he would have thought of it on his own."

"No."

"Mrs. Morley would have had to have got Dillow to do it for her," went on Crosby. "For all that she's got biggish feet for a woman she doesn't look the club-swinging sort."

"There is another possibility ..."

Crosby sighed. He wasn't good at assimilating more than two or three at a time.

Inspector Sloan tapped his notebook. "That the attack on the muniments had nothing to do with the murder of Meredith."

Crosby had not thought of this. "Coincidence?" he said doubtfully.

"Not exactly. Just two things happening on the same day."

"Matching up with the two separate discoveries, sir?" suggested Crosby brightly. "The one about the earldom ..."

"Which may or may not be true ..."

"And the one Meredith made on the Friday afternoon ..."

"Which we know nothing whatsoever about ..."

"That he tried to get in touch with the vicar to tell him?"

"Well done, Constable. Now, can you tell me the only significant thing that we know about Friday afternoon so far?"

"No," said Crosby promptly. "Nothing else happened apart from Meredith finding out something ..."

"Let's put it another way," said Sloan patiently. At this rate they'd have to call in outside help, whether Superintendent Leeyes wanted it or not. "What change in routine was there on Friday afternoon that we already know about?"

Crosby gave a short laugh. "The only thing that was different that we know about for certain sure ..."

"Yes?"

"The two old birds upstairs ..."

"Lady Alice and Lady Maude." There were moments when he would have welcomed more sophisticated assistance, too. This was one of them.

"Lady Alice and Lady Maude"—Crosby tacitly accepted the emendation. "They didn't ask the deceased to tea like they usually did on Fridays."

"Exactly, Crosby."

"You mean that is important, sir?"

"I mean"—grimly—"that that's the only positive pointer we have so far. That and the fact that William Murton has been in Ornum for all of forty-eight hours without asking his uncle for money, which I understand practically constitutes a record."

"That is unusual," admitted the Earl of Ornum. He was in the private apartments regaling a tall thin individual with something from a decanter and thin biscuits. "I think it is … er … pretty well accepted that William only retreats to Ornum when his … er … other commitments become very pressing."

The Earl had introduced Sloan and Crosby to the bleak-looking man. He was, it transpired, Mr. Adrian Cossington, the senior partner in the old established law firm of Oaten, Oaten and Cossington, and if his ascetic appearance was anything to go by, he had long ago done with all human desire and feeling. His pleasures, if any, looked as if they were confined to wrestling with "nice" legal points, or perhaps advising against the indulgences proposed by his clients.

He was obviously opposed to the Earl of Ornum saying anything to anyone at all at this stage—but especially to Inspector Sloan.

"Don't be silly, Cossington," said the Earl testily, showing more courage in dealing with the solicitor than Sloan would have dared to have done. "The fellow's got to find out who killed Meredith, hasn't he?"

"Certainly, my lord, nevertheless your own responsibilities in the matter are confined to—"

"Dammit, man, there's such a thing as justice." He turned. "Isn't there, Inspector?"

"I think so," said Sloan cautiously. Asked point-blank like that he wasn't sure that there was.

"In your own interest, my lord," protested Cossington.

"We are not considering my interest, Cossington, we are considering law and order."

That was different.

Sloan, who wasn't sure about justice, was absolutely certain about law and order. You'd got to have it or you were barbarian.

The Earl was taking his stance. "I can't have my own librarian and archivist killed in m'own house, Cossington, now, can I?"

That was what rankled, thought Sloan irrelevantly. From the Earl's point of view it was "touch my servant and you touch me." That was how it would have been in the old days. The first Earl would have had his own following, half servant, half army. Vassals, obedient to him unto death. And the Earl would have been obedient to the King, would have taken an oath of obedience at the King's coronation.

Every earl at every coronation.

Even now.

It had a name, that oath. He would remember it in a moment. An odd word … "fealty," that was it.

The solicitor had started to explain to the Earl that narrow line between obstructing the police in the execution of their duty and those tenuous circumstances in which no man need offer evidence that might incriminate himself.

Sloan wasn't listening. He was looking across at the thirteenth Earl of Ornum with new eyes. He, Charles Dennis Sloan, Detective Inspector in Her Majesty's County Constabulary of Calleshire, was the natural heir and successor to the Earl in this matter of law and order. Where once the Earl had kept unruly villains obedient so now did he. Sloan, too, had taken an oath of allegiance. And he hadn't realized until now how ancient was his duty.

The Earl of Ornum hadn't been listening to the solicitor either. "Purvis tells me you've asked the county archivist in, Inspector."

"Yes, my lord. With your permission …"

His Lordship nodded. "Meredith wouldn't have liked it, but that can't be helped. Not now. Possessive lot, these archivists. Always wanting to build their own empires. Never prepared to lend a hand with anyone else's."

"Was there anything here that anyone hankered after then?" asked Sloan suddenly. It was something he should have asked before.

The Earl thought for a moment. "Some items are always being asked for on loan."

"Which are they, my lord?"

The Earl waved a hand. "Some very early court stuff, which seems to have survived. Records of Oyer, Terminer, and Assize. That sort of thing."

One lecture, that's all they'd had when Sloan joined the force, on the history of the legal system in England. And he hadn't listened anyway.

"The old Courts of Gaol Delivery, you know," said his Lordship. "Going back a good bit now, of course. Not many of them about these days. Things have changed since then." A faint gleam of humor crept into the melancholy countenance. "Now we have you, Inspector, and Cossington over there instead of just me."

Justice instead of rough justice?

Sloan wasn't sure. He cleared his throat and came back to the point. "These records, my lord, are they worth stealing?"

"Nothing is worth stealing, Inspector."

Sloan flushed. "I'm sorry, my lord. I meant …"

The whole atmosphere in the private apartments had changed subtly. "They have a value, Inspector …"

"Yes, my lord, I'm sure …"

"But too high a value to have a price."

"I see, my lord."

"No, Inspector, you do not see. The county archivist would like them for his empire. He sees himself as the true representative of the common man—to whom he probably thinks they should belong anyway. The rate-payer incarnate."

"Quite so …"

"What was it that French fellow said …"

"I couldn't say, my lord …"

"Property is theft."

It was not a police point of view. Nor an English one, if it came to that. Property was respectable in the police world. Men without property were like gamblers without a stake, a rootless, drifting menace. Men with nothing to lose.

"The Inns of Court would like them for their empire," went on his Lordship, "because they see themselves as a profession and they think a profession can have a body. It can't. It's only as good as the worst of its members."

"Yes, my lord." As far as the aristocracy was concerned professions were doubtless new jumped-up callings.

"One of the universities wants them for their empire because they think they represent the intellectual man and that that is sufficient reason. It isn't."

"No, my lord."

"The intellectual man can be swayed by intellect …"

"Yes, my lord." Sloan had thought that was the whole idea.

"Dangerous, that."

"Very possibly, my lord." Was that the aristocrat pronouncing on the meritocrat?

"Brains," pronounced his lordship oracularly, "are all very well in their way. That right, Cossington?"

Mr. Adrian Cossington was far too clever to admit to having any at all and merely murmured, "A point of view, my lord, a point of view."

In a moment, thought Sloan, he's going to say, "My country, right or wrong."

But he didn't.

Instead the Earl said, "That's when you get political arithmetic creeping in, Inspector."

"Do you, my lord?" Sloan didn't know about political arithmetic, but he did know that the Earl was trying to convey a philosophy to him, a philosophy that did not encompass murder.

"The greatest good of the greatest number."

"I see, sir." Wasn't that known as "the common weal," or was that something different?

"And, Inspector, because they are of historical value I may not sell them to the highest bidder."

"No, my lord?"

"My country which bleeds me white does not allow me the freedom of the marketplace."

Sloan was more aware now of Cossington stirring in the background.

"All I may do, Inspector, is to retrench against a taxation system whose only aim is to deprive me of my inheritance."

"Those court records," said Sloan, policeman not politician, "would they have been in the muniments chests?"

"In the ordinary way," agreed the Earl.

"But not on Friday?" Sloan's view of Ornum was blinkered to Friday.

The Earl shook his head. "They've been on loan to the Greatorex Library since the beginning of June."

"Who all knew this?"

"Anyone who cared to read the papers," said his Lordship blandly.

"Cor," said Constable Crosby expressively as they left the private apartments, "he's agin the government if you like."

Inspector Sloan's mind was elsewhere. He was wondering if hounds felt the same sense of disappointment as he did now when they had been following a scent that turned out to be false. For a moment he had thought he had been on to something.

Crosby waved a hand. "And he calls this being bled white."

"All things are relative, Crosby."

Just how relative, though, was all this to a handful of police constables getting a few shillings' palm oil from a greedy garage proprietor every now and then?

"I'd like to have his sort of money all the same," persisted Crosby.

"No, you wouldn't." The mental dichotomy between this investigation and the other was almost too much. They were at the extreme opposite ends of the scale.

But it was the same scale.

He knew that.

And so did Superintendent Leeyes.

"Try me," said the constable cheerfully, "that's all I ask, sir."

Sloan looked across at Crosby, trying to see in him the lineal descendent of those early Earls of Ornum. Crosby suppressing tearaways on motorcycles or calming overexcited yobboes on a Saturday night or pounding the beat midweek, but that image, too, had faded now.

"I want to see Lady Alice again," he said abruptly.

As before, Lady Maude opened the door and led the way to her sister.

"Just one more question, your Ladyship," he began.

The lorgnette hovered above the Cremond beak again. "Well?"

"Who all knew you hadn't invited Mr. Meredith to tea on Friday?"

From where Sloan was standing the lorgnette magnified the beady eyes.

"Just," said her Ladyship balefully, "Mr. Meredith."

14

Miles Cremond looked as if he could have eaten any number of extra teas at any time. His overweight was of the solid, long-standing variety. He was very willing to talk to Inspector Sloan and Constable Crosby. He didn't often get an audience who hung on his every word like they did.

"Came down for the cricket," said Miles, sounding faintly aggrieved. "Not for all this business. Always come for this match. 'S'tradition."

Sloan listened carefully. What he was listening for was a clue as to why the murder had happened exactly when it did.

"I mean to say," Miles went on, "the poor old chap never did anyone any harm, did he?"

"Not that I know of, sir." Sloan went on to establish that Thursday was the first time Miles and Laura had heard about the archivist's doubts about the earldom.

"A lot of nonsense, I'm sure, Inspector," said Miles warmly. "'Course Uncle Harry's the right chap. It stands to reason …"

Sloan didn't know if primogeniture was reason.

"The rest's history, isn't it?" said Miles.

"I couldn't say, sir, I'm sure."

"A lot of families chop and change in the succession, I know, but we've been luckier than most."

"Really, sir?"

"Because of this thing about battles, what?"

"What thing?"

"Never getting there," said Miles. "Whenever there's been a war the Cremonds always seem to have been either too old or too young to fight, what?"

"The General …" said Sloan suddenly, remembering the bust in the library.

"That's right. Him, too. I think one of the other Cremonds got to Blenheim, but his gout held him back from the actual fighting, what?"

"Quite so, sir." Where Sloan came from, the word "what" was a simple interrogative. This man used it like a full stop. "Now, about Friday, sir …"

120

"Yes?"

"Where were you at the material … at teatime on Friday?"

"Had a quick cup with the others."

"The others?"

"Uncle Harry, Aunt Millicent, Henry and Eleanor, Cousin Gertrude, and m'wife. I didn't stay with them more than five minutes. I wanted to get out-of-doors and Cousin Gertrude wanted to get back to her chandelier, so we went."

"What sort of time would this have been, sir?"

He frowned. "I must have been heading for the ha ha by ten past four."

"I beg your pardon, sir?"

"The ha ha."

"That's what I thought you said." Sloan tried it out for himself. Tentatively. "The ha ha?"

"That's right, Inspector."

"And what"—cautiously—"did you do when you got there?"

"Walked round it."

"I see, sir." It was like one of those radio parlor games where everyone else knew the object. He suppressed an urge to say, "Can you eat it?" Instead he murmured, "Did you see anyone while you were there?"

Miles Cremond frowned again. "Purvis. He was talking to Bert Hackle by the orangery."

Sloan sighed. It was altogether too simple to suppose that you kept oranges there. "Anyone else?"

"No, Inspector."

"And when did you get back?"

"Late."

"Late? Late for what?"

"Dinner, Inspector. I'd hardly left myself time to change. M'wife was waiting for me and we went down together a bit late."

"And you were walking all the time, sir?"

"Yes, Inspector."

"Round the ha ha?"

"Yes."

"Very funny," said Crosby not quite inaudibly enough.

"What's that?" Miles Cremond jerked forward.

"Nothing, sir," interposed Sloan smoothly. "Now, was there anything else you can tell us about Friday?"

But the Honorable Miles Cremond couldn't think of anything out of the ordinary that had happened on Friday, or any other day for that matter.

The whole business was a complete mystery to him, what?

So it was too, apparently, to his wife, Laura.

She did, however, think any discoveries of Osborne Meredith's about the earldom were perfectly absurd.

"Perfectly absurd," she repeated for good measure.

"You didn't take them seriously, you mean, madam?"

"I didn't, Inspector."

"It seems," said Sloan mildly, "as if someone did."

There was no denying that someone—someone wearing a woman's shoe, size six and a half—had taken them seriously enough to have a real go at disturbing the muniments.

He said so.

"But," protested Laura, "but you couldn't take all this away and give it to someone else." She waved a hand in a comprehensive gesture that included house, park, and—somehow—earldom.

"I couldn't," agreed Sloan. "There would have to be a successful claimant through the law courts."

"But," she wailed, "we don't even know who the claimant would be."

"No?" Sloan would have to try to work out the significance of that later. "Mr. Meredith would presumably have known."

It seemed Laura Cremond had not thought of this.

"He might," suggested Sloan, "have been the only person who did know."

She lifted her head sharply at this. There was nothing Cremond about her at all, noted Sloan. Just the touch of fast-fading handsomeness and a good hairdresser.

"You mean," she ventured cautiously, "that now he's dead we may never know?"

"I couldn't say, madam, at this stage. He may have left a written note."

"No"—quickly.

Too quickly.

"No, madam?"

"I mean"—she flushed—"not that anyone knew about."

"He might have communicated the result of his researches to someone outside the family." Sloan's eyes drifted downwards in the direction of her shoes. He said austerely, "Tell me again about Friday afternoon, madam, please."

She was beginning to look flustered. "There's nothing to tell, Inspector. I went to my room after tea—there wasn't anything else to do really. Cousin Gertrude had gone off to finish her chandelier, Uncle Harry always has a little sleep just about then, and my husband had gone for a walk."

"Lord Henry and Lady Eleanor?"

"They went down to Ornum village to see their old nanny—she's not been well."

"And the Countess?" It was like a roll-call.

"Aunt Millicent?" Laura Cremond said waspishly, "You can't really have a conversation with Aunt Millicent."

"No"—Sloan supposed you couldn't. Any more than you could talk to a butterfly. He murmured, "I see, madam. So you went to your room?"

"That's right, Inspector."

"And stayed there?"

"Yes, Inspector."

Sloan looked down at her for a long moment, and then said soberly, "I think you have had a lucky escape, madam. A very lucky escape indeed."

Talking to Lady Eleanor Cremond was a refreshing change. Sloan could quite understand why Charles Purvis was smitten.

She was all that a good witness should be.

Simple, direct, sure without being categoric.

"I saw Ossy just before four o'clock," she repeated.

"Alive and well?"

"Very well, Inspector, if you know what I mean. Almost excited."

"About what?"

"He didn't tell me. We just chatted for a moment or two, then I took a book and went away." She paused. "He was a real enthusiast, you know."

"Yes." That hadn't saved him. Almost the reverse, you might say. He watched her closely. "His tea?"

"No, I didn't stay for that. I asked him to join us as he wasn't going up to the great-aunts, but he said he had something he wanted to do and he was expecting Mr. Ames any minute."

Teatime on Friday had suddenly become immensely important.

Lady Eleanor, though, was thinking about luncheon today.

"You must be famished," she said, looking at her watch. "I'll get Dillow to bring you something. Where will you be?"

"Thank you, that would be kind, your Ladyship. The armory …"

"You don't want to eat there, Inspector." She thought for a moment. "I know the very place. The gun room."

The gun room it was. As appropriate a murder headquarters as anyone could meet.

"They've got weapons on the brain here, that's their trouble," grumbled Crosby, looking round the small room, which was literally lined with guns. "Look at 'em. I should have thought they'd have got enough downstairs without this little lot."

"With one notable exception," Sloan reminded him. "Those downstairs are ornamental. These are for use."

The guns showed every sign of having as much loving care expended on them as did the china.

"Those deer that the Earl's so keen about," said Crosby.

"Yes?"

"Does he shoot them?"

"He breeds them first," said Sloan.

"Then he shoots them?"

"I expect so."

Crosby scratched his forehead. "Funny lot, the aristocracy, sir, aren't they?"

"Government by the best citizens, Constable, that's what it means." Sloan took out his pen and got back to business. "It's one weapon on one brain that's our trouble, you know."

Dillow brought them welcome beer and sandwiches, and was word perfect about what he'd said before.

"No, sir, I was not aware until I took tea to their Ladyships upstairs that Mr. Meredith was not taking tea with them as usual on Fridays."

"What time would that have been?" Sloan discovered there was one exception to the rule that policemen called all other men "sir." That was when the other chap got it in first.

"About half-past three, sir. They like it early on account of their taking a short nap after luncheon."

"Thank you, Dillow."

The phrase constituted dismissal to a butler and Dillow left them.

They went on working while they ate. Inspector Sloan turned over a fresh sheet in his notebook. Outside the window a peacock shrilled harshly.

"Why doesn't he shoot them instead?" muttered Crosby indistinctly.

"They're another sort of ornament, that's why."

"Give me the gryphons any day." Crosby took another sandwich. "At least they don't make a noise."

Sloan stared at the blank page in front of him. "Now then, how far have we got?"

"Nowhere," said Crosby.

"We know who the victim is," said Sloan patiently. That was a head start on some of the cases he'd been on. "And we know where we think he was killed."

"Sitting down at the table at the far end of the library," agreed Crosby. "Confirmed as probable by the forensic people."

"How nearly do we know when?" The inductive method, that's what this was called. Crosby didn't seem much good at the deductive sort.

"After Lady Eleanor and Dillow saw him about four o'clock."

"But before he'd had time to eat his tea."

"Unless they're both lying, sir," said Crosby assiduously.

"True."

"We don't know why he was killed." Crosby was making good headway with the sandwiches.

"Half-why," said Sloan, taking one himself while they were still there to take. "He'd found out something somebody didn't want him to know. Mrs. Ames confirms the telephone call, by the way, but you must check on the vicar's movements before five-thirty."

"I have," said Crosby unexpectedly. "I had a word with the postmistress. She knows everything. He was in the village until just before half-past five. She saw him going in and out of houses."

Sloan nodded. "So we know when—within limits."

"But we don't really know why, sir, do we?" Pessimistically.

"We know where."

"But we don't know who." Crosby took the last sandwich. "These are jolly good, sir, aren't they?"

"They were," said Sloan sarcastically. He was wasting his time.

"We know who it wasn't, though, sir, don't we?" mumbled Crosby, undeterred by a mouthful of sandwich.

"Oh?"

"It wasn't the Earl and Countess because they were together in the drawing room from teatime onwards."

"There might have been collusion between them. They're husband and wife, remember ..."

Crosby frowned. "I shouldn't care to collude—colluse—what you said, sir—with the Countess myself. Too risky. Anyway, their son and daughter didn't leave them until about twenty past four and I bet old Meredith would have got his teeth into his tea by then if he'd been alive to do it."

"Like you fell upon your lunch just now?"

"Well, sir, he wouldn't have just sat looking at it, would he?"

"I agree it's unlikely."

"And if the Honorable Miles is speaking the truth ..."

"If ..."

"Purvis and Hackle were together completely outside the house."

"That leaves ..." Sloan started to write.

"Cousin Gertrude, who was on the loose ..."

That was one way of putting it.

"Miles himself," said Crosby. "He could have seen the two others from a window."

Sloan nodded. "Make a note to ask them if they saw him."

"William Murton, who may or who may not have been in Ornum."

"And Dillow," said Sloan.

"Four suspects," concluded Crosby, recapping. "Cousin Gertrude, Miles, William, and Dillow."

"While we're reconstructing the crime," said Sloan, "let's go on with what happened after."

"After, sir?"

"It can't have escaped your notice, Crosby, that the body wasn't found in the library."

"No, sir."

"Well, then ..."

"Somebody removed it from the library."

"Well done. The murderer, would you think? Or did someone come along and tidy it away just to be helpful?"

"Unlikely, that, sir."

"Of course it's unlikely," snapped Sloan. Sarcasm was a real boomerang of a weapon. He should have remembered that. He went on more peaceably, "The murderer moved it to the armory ..."

"Yes, sir, but they didn't put it straight into the armor, did they, because of rigor mortis. The doctor said so."

Sloan tapped his notebook. "Now I wonder when he did that."

"Dead of night?" suggested Crosby brightly.

"Leaving the body from four o'clock onwards in the library."

"Risky," agreed Crosby.

"But not desperately risky. They don't strike one as great readers here. . . . Crosby."

Crosby was engaged in draining the beer bottle to the very last drop. "Sir?"

"Think."

"Yes, sir."

"The muniments come into this somewhere. I wish I knew how."

"Whoever did the muniments," offered Crosby after a little thought, "did them after Meredith had been ... er ... done."

"I grant you that," said Sloan immediately. "Meredith wouldn't have stood for that. When were the muniments disturbed?"

"We don't know, sir." There was positively no beer left now.

Sloan dropped his pen onto his notebook. "There's no end to the things we don't know. What we want, Crosby, is someone who went into the library that evening."

"Or someone who saw the murderer carrying the body to the armory," said Crosby helpfully.

Sloan looked at him for a minute and slowly picked up his pen again. "We've got that, haven't we, Constable?"

"Have we, sir?"

"Don't you remember?"

Crosby stared. "No, sir."

"Someone saw somebody in the great hall, don't you remember?"

"No, sir."

"Just before dinner, Crosby, on Friday"—with mounting excitement. "After the dressing bell had gone. While everyone in the house could reasonably be expected to be dressing for dinner in their own rooms."

Light began to dawn on Crosby's face. "You don't mean ..."

"I do. Lady Alice Cremond saw ..."

"Judge Cremond ..."

"Exactly."

"But he's a ghost."

Sloan sighed. "Do you believe in ghosts, Constable?"

"No, sir."

"Neither do I. I'm prepared to bet that what the old lady saw—without her lorgnette, mind you—was not a sixteenth-century ghost at all, but a twentieth-century murderer carrying the body of a small man."

It was Police Constable Albert Bloggs who disturbed them.

Dillow brought him to the gun room.

"He said you were here, sir," said Bloggs, jerking a thumb at Dillow's departing back. "I didn't know whether to come straight here or to ring through to the station."

"What about, Bloggs?" asked Sloan warily.

"That young chap, Murton, sir, who I was watching ..."

"Go on."

"He's gone and given me the slip."

15

"Find him," commanded Superintendent Leeyes briefly over the telephone.

"Yes, sir," said Sloan.

"And quickly."

"Yes, sir."

"Where did he go missing?"

"Here," said Sloan miserably.

"What!" exploded Leeyes. "You mean he's on the loose somewhere in that ruddy great house and you don't know where?"

"Yes, sir. Bloggs tailed him after lunch from his cottage in the village up here to the house, and then Murton went round the back somewhere and Bloggs lost him."

"Bloggs lost him," repeated Leeyes nastily. "Just like that. A child of ten could probably have kept him in sight. It's very nearly Midsummer's Day, Sloan, it's not even dusk let alone dark and he lost him."

"Yes, sir."

"So I suppose Bloggs went round to the front door and rang the bell."

"More or less," admitted Sloan unhappily. He didn't really see what else Bloggs could have done but that.

"And what has Murton come up to the house for, Sloan? Have you thought about that?"

"Yes, sir." Sloan had in fact been thinking about very little else since Bloggs had arrived at the gun room. "I don't know, sir, but I'm worried."

"So am I," said Superintendent Leeyes from the detached comfort of his own office in Berebury Police Station. "Very."

The Countess of Ornum poured a second cup of coffee for Mr. Adrian Cossington. It was practically cold and he hadn't asked for it anyway, but he didn't complain. Luncheon had been over for some time and a general move away from the drawing room was in the air.

"I'd like you to take a look at the herd, Cossington," said the Earl. "A good year, I think after all. You sometimes get it after a bad winter."

"Certainly, my lord. I shall look forward to that." The very last thing the City solicitor wanted to do was to plod across the park after the Earl hoping to catch a glimpse of the fleeting shy creatures. Legally speaking—and Mr. Cossington rarely spoke or thought otherwise—deer were not particularly interesting to him. Being *ferae naturae* there was no private property in them or common law crime in killing them.

"Just the thing after a meal, a good walk in the park," observed the Earl.

"Very pleasant, my lord." Cossington was still automatically considering the legal aspects of deer. The only remedy against having your own deer killed was to prevent trespass in pursuit of them or to punish the trespasser.

The Earl rose. "When you've finished your coffee, then, Cossington."

The solicitor hastily swallowed the trepid fluid. Ordinarily he liked a certain amount of sang froid in his clients, but the aristocracy were inclined to carry things a little too far.

"Are you coming, too, Henry?" asked his father.

"Er ... no. 'Fraid not. Got to get the car straightened out, you know. Thanks all the same."

"Eleanor?"

"All right, I'll come."

Cousin Gertrude got to her feet and said heavily, "Well, this won't do. I've got work to do."

"Poor Gertrude," said the Countess sympathetically, "you're always so busy."

"Someone's got to do the flowers," she said. "They haven't been touched since Friday what with one thing and another."

"Mostly one thing, what?" blurted Miles.

She ignored him. "Hackle brought some fresh flowers in this morning. That's one thing you can say for the month of June. There's no shortage of flowers."

"And no shortage of vases," observed the Countess, "so that's all right."

"Quite," said Gertrude stiffly. "Quite."

Mr. Adrian Cossington felt constrained to say something about the murder. "Are you making any changes in ... er ... routine since ... er ... yesterday's discovery, my lord?"

The Earl stared. "Changes? Here?"

"Yes, my lord."

"No."

Cossington tried again. "The public, my lord. Are they still to be admitted as usual?"

"Certainly."

"Is that wise, my lord?"

"Wise?"

"The murder ..."

"If they want their vicarious bread and circuses, Cossington, I see no reason to stop them."

"You'll have a good crowd."

"You think so? Good."

"Culture vultures in the long gallery," said Lord Henry.

"Eager beavers in the great hall," chimed in Lady Eleanor.

"And aesthete's foot by the time they get to Cousin Gertrude in the china room," added Lord Henry.

"How disgusting that sounds," said the Countess. She turned to a hitherto rather silent Miles and Laura. "What are you two going to do?"

Laura said that she had a splitting headache and was going to lie down, and that Miles was going out for a walk.

"He needs some air," she said.

"Just like Friday," observed Cousin Gertrude.

"Not like Friday at all," retorted Laura.

Gertrude grunted. "No, of course not. That was exercise he wanted then, wasn't it?"

"He got it," said Laura pointedly, "but not by killing old Mr. Meredith."

"Just by walking in the park, what?" said Miles.

The Countess made a vague gesture in the direction of the coffee pot, but no one took her up on this. "Has anyone remembered to feed the little man from county hall?"

Lady Eleanor said, "I told Dillow, Mother. And about the police."

Mention of the police started Adrian Cossington off again. "My lord, are you sure that it is prudent to open the house again so soon ..."

"I think," said the Earl, encompassing a whole philosophy, "one should always carry on as usual."

"A few changes might well be indicated, my lord. As your legal adviser ..."

"When it is not necessary to change," quoted the Earl sententiously, "it is necessary not to change. I think you may take it, Cossington, that things are back to normal now."

They weren't.

Not from the view of Sloan and Crosby and the luckless Bloggs.

Sloan had barely got back from the gun room when a police motorcyclist arrived from Berebury with a sheaf of reports.

The pathologist's official one, marked "Copy to H.M. Coroner": the facts of death in the language of academe. Brutality smoothed down to detached observation.

A note from aforementioned H.M. Coroner appointing Thursday for the inquest.

A dry comment from the forensic laboratory: the blood from the spine of the book in the library complied with all the accepted tests with that of the deceased. The hairs on the instrument known as Exhibit B ...

"What's Exhibit A?" said Sloan suddenly.

"A for armor," said Crosby, who had done the labelling.

And B for blunt instrument? Sloan didn't ask.

Exhibit B resembled that of deceased under all the known comparison indices. So did the blood on Exhibit B. An attempt had been made to wipe it clean. There were no fingerprints.

Two reports from London whence enquiries had been put in hand about Miles Cremond and William Murton.

The Pedes Shipping Line was nearly on the rocks. It was suspected that the name of the Honorable Miles Cremond was included on the board of directors solely to lend an air of credulity to the operations of the company. If, the writer of the report put it graphically, the inspector was thinking of making an investment, the South Sea Bubble would be a better bet.

William Murton lived at the address stated, which was a bed-sitter-cum-studio, and apparently possessed two characteristics unfortunate in combination—expensive tastes and a low income.

"Living it up without having anything to live on," said Crosby, who wouldn't have dared.

"Except his uncle," said Sloan. "I reckon he lives on him."

"I don't know why he lets him, sir, honestly I don't. My uncle ..."

"It's called noblesse oblige."

It would seem, went on the compiler of the report, a man with a taste for a good phrase, that William Murton pursues his career in fits and starts and nubile young ladies all of the time.

Near the bottom of the sheaf was a scribbled note from Inspector Harpe of Traffic Division begging Sloan to come to see him as soon as he possibly could.

Sloan slipped that one into his inside jacket pocket. If there was anything approaching natural selection in troubles it was their tendency to multiply at the wrong time.

There was also a communication from the policeman who had interviewed the executors of the late Mr. Beresford Baggles to the effect that Michael Joseph Dillow had worked for Mr. Baggles until the latter's death from apoplexy. Dillow had been left the sum of five hundred pounds by

Mr. Baggles, being in his employ and not under notice at the time of Mr. Baggles' death.

The legacy had not yet been paid out owing to the difficulties encountered by the executors on the discovery that Mr. Baggles' considerable collection of the works of the artist Van Gogh were fakes (which discovery had occasioned the apoplexy), but that Dillow would be receiving it as soon as the estate was wound up.

"Van Gogh," murmured Sloan. "That's the chap who cut off his ear, isn't it?"

P.C. Bloggs, who in another day and age would doubtless have had both his ears chopped off for him, remained silent.

Crosby sniffed. "Funny fellows, painters."

Which brought them back to William Murton.

"It'll take an army to find him in this place," said Crosby, thinking aloud. "There's I don't know how many rooms ..."

"Just under three hundred," said Sloan.

"And what's to stop him dashing from one to the other while you're searching?"

"Nothing," agreed Sloan wearily. "Nothing at all. However, reinforcements are on the way."

On the terrace outside the gun room window a peacock shrieked derisively.

Bert Hackle was carrying a wooden board. "Will this do, Mr. Purvis?"

The steward measured it with his eye. "That's about right, Bert, thank you. Now let's see if it'll fit."

Charles Purvis had in his hand a stout sheet of white card on which he had been laboring for a tidy effect. On it had been printed as neatly as possible ARMORY 2/6d EXTRA.

"Very nice," said Hackle, who was a great admirer of the Earl.

"It's not the same as a printed notice, of course," murmured Purvis, standing back to see the effect, "but there isn't time to have it done properly by Wednesday."

Hackle jerked his shoulder towards the top of the armory stairs. "Reckon they'll let us in there again b'Wednesday?"

"His Lordship does," Charles Purvis looked round. "Now to find something to put the board on."

"What we want," said Bert, "is a proper stand." By rights Bert Hackle shouldn't have been in the great hall at all in his gardening boots, but as there had been Hackles in Ornum village almost as long as there had been Cremonds in Ornum House—though not so well-documented—he was privileged in his own right. He creaked across the floor looking for something suitable. "If we was to lean it up against this we'd be all right."

"Not if Mr. Feathers saw us," retorted Purvis smartly. "That's his best piece of ormolu on malachite, that is."

Hackle, whose interest in minerals was confined to the rocks in the rockery, tried again. "What about that box thing?"

That box thing was satinwood inlaid with ivory and contained the ceremonial trowel with which his Lordship the eleventh had cut the first turf for the first railway line to link Luston and Berebury. (It had been a singularly happy occasion as his Lordship, being the owner of all the suitable land in between these two places, had been able to name his own price. And had.)

"Much better," said Purvis. "Now, if you'll just heave that table a bit nearer the doorway."

Standing on the table and propped against the satinwood box the notice was now eminently readable.

Mr. Robert Hamilton did not accord with Inspector Sloan's conception of the common man.

The county archivist was exceedingly spry, erudite, and helpful.

Inspector Sloan, being in the position of having a force too meager to be worth deploying, had taken it with him to the muniments room. Insofar as the murder of Osborne Meredith had a focal point it was in this part of the house.

"Ah, Inspector ..." Mr. Hamilton looked up. "Come in. I don't think we can say you'll disturb anything any more than it's been disturbed already."

"No. Have you had any visitors here, sir, so far?"

"Yes, indeed, Inspector. A Miss Gertrude Cremond came along to see if she could help, a Mrs. Laura Cremond, who thought something of hers might be in here, and the butler."

"Dillow?"

"Is that his name? He left me something to eat in the library, but I asked him to bring it here instead."

"Not William Murton?" Sloan described the missing man. "You haven't seen him?"

Hamilton shook his head, while Sloan glanced round the room.

"Someone," observed Mr. Hamilton profoundly, "was wanting to impede research here."

"Yes."

"It'll take a week or more to go through"—Robert Hamilton waved a hand at the chaotic papers—"and restore even the semblance of order—quite apart from finding whatever it is I'm supposed to be looking for in here." He cocked his head alertly. "You can't give me even a small clue as to what that can be?"

Sloan shook his head. "All we know is that someone stirred them up and that someone tried to get in here last night after we'd sealed the door."

"Ah, well there's no wilful damage that I can see, and that's something—for there's as pretty a collection of documents here as you could hope to find. Nor theft, I should say at a quick guess."

"No."

"Someone ignorant," added Mr. Hamilton. "Someone plain ignorant."

"A woman," said Sloan. "We have reason to believe it was a woman."

"Ah," said the archivist, "that explains it. They seemed to be aiming at mayhem."

"I think," said Sloan slowly, "that they were aiming at making it difficult for anyone to prove that the Earl of Ornum isn't the Earl."

"Yes," said the archivist unexpectedly. "The poor fellow wrote me about that a week or so back."

"He did?" Sloan sat up.

"He was mistaken, of course," declared Mr. Hamilton. "I can assure you, Inspector, the succession is perfectly sound. Perfectly."

"But Mr. Meredith thought …"

"He made a common mistake. He was misled by a case of *mort d'ancestor* in the family. Tricky, of course."

"You mean …"

"And he was also a wee bit confused about socage."

Sloan was aware of Crosby's head coming up like a pointer.

"Socage," repeated Sloan carefully.

"That's right, Inspector. Common socage. Meredith was all right in his facts, but a bit out in his inferences. He was," said the utterly professional Robert Hamilton, "an amateur. A good amateur, mind you, I will say that, but not a trained man."

"He hadn't told anyone he had been mistaken," said Sloan, trying to assimilate the news and place it in the pattern of the crime.

"Now, Inspector"—Hamilton smiled faintly—"there's not many people in a hurry to do that, is there?"

"True," agreed Sloan. Better though, perhaps, to admit a mistake and keep your skull intact. "This socage, Mr. Hamilton …"

"The tenure of land other than by knight-service."

Why was it, thought Sloan, that no one would explain things to him in words that he understood?

"Knight-service?" he echoed wearily.

"That's right," said the amiable Mr. Hamilton. "Estates like these came directly from the crown in the beginning in return for services rendered ... usually men at arms in times of war."

That explained the armory if not the gun room.

"You see, Inspector, in theory all land belongs to the King or Queen as the case may be."

"Not still?" said Sloan, thinking of his roses, and his neat semidetached house in suburban Berebury.

"Yes." The archivist chuckled. "I daresay you're of an age to have done your own knight-service yourself, Inspector."

Sloan hadn't thought of it in that light before, but ...

"Not quite the same thing," admitted Hamilton, "but not all that far away. That's where the Earldom came in. Men who brought their armies with them to the King's wars. They were made Earls—"

"The rest," interrupted the unconscionable Constable Crosby triumphantly, "were churls."

It was not often that Charles Purvis was caught on the wrong foot. He was a naturally competent man, unobtrusively given to attending to detail. Even the distraction of admiring the adorable Lady Eleanor from afar did not normally cause his work to suffer.

But, as it was subsequently agreed, a murder in the house was enough to put any man off his stroke, to drive less important matters out of mind.

So it was that when a coach drew up at the front door of Ornum House at exactly three o'clock he was all prepared to send it away. True, it was not quite the same as the sort of coach that usually came to the house on open days. It was infinitely more luxurious; and it did not proclaim the fact in letters a foot high.

Charles Purvis saw the coach from the great hall and as Dillow for once did not seem to be about he went himself to the door.

"I'm very sorry," he began firmly, "but the house is not open today ..."

"Mr. Purvis?"

Charles Purvis found his hand being crushed in a vice-like grip.

"I'm Fortescue, Mr. Purvis. Cromwell T. Fortescue. You wrote me ..."

"I did?" Purvis blinked.

"You sure did. You wrote me, Mr. Purvis, to say we might see the Earl's pictures today. We're the Young Masters Art Society."

Hot on the wheels of this coach came another one.

Nothing like as luxurious as the first, it had been commandeered by Superintendent Leeyes to convey as many of his force as he could drum up to Ornum House to assist Inspector Sloan in the hunt for William Murton.

It took their concerted efforts, directed by Inspector Sloan and aided by Police Constables Crosby and Bloggs, about an hour to find him.

In the *oubliette*.

Dead.

16

"He can't be," bellowed Superintendent Leeyes.

"He is, sir. I'm very sorry ..."

"I should think so, Sloan. You haven't heard the last of this. If Bloggs hadn't lost him ..."

Sloan forbore to point out that Constable Bloggs had been watching William Murton for a totally different reason.

"And, Sloan, if you had got on to him quicker then this wouldn't have happened ..."

"No, sir. Dr. Dabbe says that's not so. He thinks he was killed as soon as he got to the house."

"Just after Bloggs lost him," pointed out Leeyes inexorably.

"It means, sir, that someone was ready for him."

"I know that, Sloan. You don't have to tell me."

"No, sir."

"Ready and waiting," snapped Leeyes.

"Yes, sir."

"With"—on a rising note—"three able-bodied policemen actually in the house at the time."

"Yes, sir." It was no good explaining that Ornum wasn't a house but a *House*, that it wasn't a two up and two down jerry-builder's delight. Or that medieval dungeons were soundproofed as a careless in-built extra.

"That doesn't make it look any better on paper either," grumbled Leeyes.

"No, sir." Nothing could make that poor distorted face look any better now either, Sloan knew that. William Murton, half gentleman, half painter, father but not husband, nephew but never heir, penniless but never properly penurious, had gone to another world where presumably all things were wholly good or wholly bad.

"And who killed him, Sloan? Tell me that."

Sloan backtracked. "Up until this afternoon, sir, we had four suspects for the murder of Mr. Osborne Meredith. William Murton was one of them."

"We are not, I hope," remarked Leeyes coldly, "playing elimination games."

"No, sir. Leaving out Murton …"

"Suicides don't strangle themselves as a rule."

"Quite so, sir"—hastily. "As you say, leaving out Murton we would have had three suspects for the first murder."

Sloan wasn't a bardolator—wouldn't even have known the meaning of the word—but he had once been to see a performance of *Macbeth*. It had been the insouciant irony of the cast list that he had remembered, could quote to this day:

Lords, Gentlemen, Officers, Soldier, Murderers, Attendants, and Messengers.

Give or take a soldier or two he reckoned they'd got the lot at Ornum today.

First and Second Murderers, there had been in the play?

Was there going to prove to have been a First Murderer for Osborne Meredith and a Second Murderer for William Murton?

Doubtful.

Or a First and Second Murderer for each as in the play?

A husband and wife? That most committing of all partnerships at law. My wife and I are one and I am he, the books said. With Miles and Laura Cremond it would be the other way round. There was no doubt there who wore the kilt.

Three suspects were two too many for Superintendent Leeyes and he said so.

"Can't you do better than that, Sloan?"

"Not at the moment, sir. Miss Gertrude Cremond, Mr. and Mrs. Miles Cremond, and Dillow could all have committed the first murder."

"And which did?"

"I don't know, sir. Of course, the second murder puts a different complexion on things. . . ."

As soon as the word was out of his mouth Sloan wished he had chosen another one instead.

Any word but complexion.

William Murton's had been hideous. A mottled reddish-blue with swollen tongue protuberant between discolored lips.

Dr. Dabbe, recalled at great speed from Berebury, had been terse.

"Strangulation," he had said at his first glance. "Not more than two hours ago at the outside. Something thin pulled over his head from behind and then tightened. I don't know what. I'll have to tell you later."

Sloan didn't know what either. The instrument of death had disappeared between swollen, engorged folds of skin. He hadn't realized the frightening vulnerability of the human neck. That a large and powerful young man like William Murton could be done to death with a quick twist of something thin round the throat seemed all wrong.

After luncheon.

Everyone in the house had dispersed after luncheon. Sloan had established that easily enough.

Then what?

Enter First Murderer for Second Murder?

"And why kill him anyway?" The Superintendent's question came charging into his train of thought.

"I don't know ..." began Sloan—and stopped.

He did know.

Something at the back of his mind told him.

It teased his subconscious. Still nominally listening to Superintendent Leeyes, he flipped back the pages of his notebook. Somewhere this morning—it couldn't only have been this morning surely—it seemed aeons ago—William Murton had said something to him which ...

He found the place in his notebook.

"I don't," William Murton had said, and he, Sloan, had written down, "earn my keep like Cousin Gertrude cleaning chandeliers for dear life. I'm a sponger."

How did William Murton, who was supposed not to have come up to Ornum House at all on Friday, know that Cousin Gertrude had been cleaning a chandelier all day? Something must have put it into his mind.

Not just "a chandelier," of course, but the great hall chandelier.

That same great hall where towards evening the ancient and ageing Lady Alice Cremond had seen what she fondly took to be the ghost of her long departed ancestor, Judge Cremond.

To know that Cousin Gertrude had been cleaning the chandelier one would have had either to see her doing it or see the pieces of crystal on the table and know that this was one of the duties arrogated to herself by the formidable Miss Cremond. Or, perhaps, as a very long shot, have talked to someone who had mentioned it.

But if William Murton had been in the house on Friday after all, why hadn't he said so?

There was one simple and very sinister to that question. Was it because William Murton had seen that same figure and not only known it not to have been Judge Cremond but had—dangerously—recognized it?

"A pikestaff ..." Superintendent Leeyes was saying.

"I beg your pardon, sir?" Cousin Gertrude was as plain as a pikestaff; was that what he meant?

"A pikestaff," repeated Leeyes irritably. "Was he killed with something fancy from the armory?"

"No, sir," dully. "The armory's locked. It'll have been something more modern than that."

Dr. Dabbe still hadn't established what by the time Sloan got back to the *oubliette*.

It was a macabre setting for murder. Death went well with bare stone and it was the little crowd of modern men who looked incongruous.

Crosby was there and a considerably shaken Bert Hackle. He it had been who had led the police search party to this part of the house, who had given a quick jerk at the *oubliette* grating without considering for a single second that there might be anything at all within—still less the crumpled heap that had been William Murton.

The Reverend Walter Ames was somehow also of this party. Sloan didn't know whether he hadn't gone home after this morning or had gone and come back again and he was too busy to care.

Dr. Dabbe was still the central figure in the drama with the others playing supporting roles. Doctors, realized Sloan, were like that.

All three professions had something to tell the police inspector.

Rather like *The Ballad of Reading Gaol*, thought Sloan, who in his day had been what is known as "good at school." His schooling had been of a vintage that had included—nay insisted—on the learning of verse by rote.

"Murton ..." began Detective Constable Crosby, "shouldn't have been in the house at all by rights."

("The governor was strong upon the regulations act.")

"If he'd stayed at home," said the law flatly, "he'd have been all right."

"The deceased," pronounced Dr. Dabbe, "was attacked from behind and died very quickly."

("The doctor said that death was but a scientific fact.")

"He struggled," observed medicine, "but it didn't do him any good."
"God rest his soul," murmured the Reverend Walter Ames.

("And twice a day the chaplain called, And left a little tract.")

"Perhaps," suggested the church gently, "in the fullness of time we shall be better able to see his life in true perspective."

Was this man of God comforting him, too, wondered Sloan? P.C. Bloggs couldn't properly be blamed for this death, but could he, Sloan? The superintendent would blame everybody, he always did, so that, working for him, you had yourself to work out where real responsibility lay.

As for perspective it was like looking down the wrong end of a telescope. Far away lay a greatly diminished figure ...

Dr. Dabbe was going now. "I've seen all I need here, Inspector. Send him back to Berebury and I'll be getting on with the post-mortem for you."

"Thank you, Doctor."

The pathologist poked a bony finger towards the *oubliette*.

"Forgotten," he said pungently, "but not gone."

He should have worked all this out before now.

Before William Murton died.

Sloan took Crosby with him to see their Ladyships upstairs. Now that the house was really full of police he thought he could leave the *oubliette* for a while.

Lady Maude answered his knock and the two policemen trooped in. It was quite impossible to tell if any hasty harbinger of bad tidings had told the two old ladies about their great-nephew William. Sloan himself had broken the news to the Earl and Countess first, and then to the rest of the family. As he had expected, Lord Henry and Lady Eleanor had been most upset.

With the two old ladies, though, it was as if a lifetime of keeping the upper lip stiff meant that it could no longer bend.

"William ..." he began tentatively.

Lady Alice inclined her head. "Millicent has told us. We expected something, you know. The Judge was about."

The chair Sloan had been given was hard and straight-backed. He twisted on it uncomfortably, unsure of what to say next. "He shouldn't have died ..."

The old, old face was inscrutable. "We've all got to die, Mr. Sloan—some of us sooner than others."

"Yes, your Ladyship," he agreed readily, "but he was young."

Sloan was struck by a sadder thought still. Perhaps, seen from Lady Alice's vantage point, a lost middle age was not something to mourn and that, as for old age—you could keep it.

"Poor boy," said Lady Maude. She, Sloan was sure, would have a lace-edged handkerchief somewhere and would shed a private tear for the dead William.

Lady Alice was made of sterner stuff.

She leaned forward. "Tell me, Mr. Sloan, do you read Boccaccio?"

"No, your Ladyship." He had a vague recollection that was the name of one of the authors that some public libraries did not stock, but he was probably mistaken.

"He put it very well for us all."

Sloan waited.

" 'Many valiant men and many fine ladies,' " she rumbled, " 'breakfasted with their kinsfolk and that same night supped with their ancestors in the other world.' "

Sloan cleared his throat. In a way, that wasn't so very far removed from what he had come about.

"Your Ladyship, can you remember Friday afternoon?"

"Of course."

"Teatime?"

"Yes?"

"How many cups were there on the tea tray?"

But in the end it was Lady Maude who remembered, not Lady Alice at all.

"Only two, Mr. Sloan, because we hadn't invited Mr. Meredith, you see."

Sloan and Crosby were walking down the great staircase together.

"We know when, Crosby."

"Yes, sir."

"We know where, Crosby."

"Yes, sir."

"And now we know who, Crosby."

"Yes, sir."

The dialogue was as rhythmical as their steps down the stair treads.

"We still don't know why."

"No, sir. Murton …"

"William Murton had to die."

"Yes, sir."

"He came up to the house on Friday evening though he told us he didn't …"

"Yes, sir."

"And saw something."

"It didn't do him any good."

"Ah, but he thought it was going to, though," said Sloan sadly. "He made the mistake of thinking he was on to a good thing."

"And so he came up to the house today …"

"Tricky business, blackmail," murmured Sloan ruminatively. "I don't think our William can have been quite up to it. He should have stuck to the Earl. He would have seen him through."

There was somebody coming along the upper landing behind them and hurrying down the stairs after them. A man's voice called out, "Inspector!"

Sloan turned.

Charles Purvis was descending on them as quickly as he could. "Inspector!"

"Yes?"

"I've just been taking the Young Masters Art Society round. They'd arranged to come and I forgot to cancel them what with one thing and another ..."

"Yes?" prompted Sloan.

"So when they came just now rather than send them away I took them round myself."

Quite obviously Charles Purvis hadn't heard about the dead William Murton yet.

"They'd come all the way from London and anyway they didn't know about Mr. Meredith ..."

"Well?"—expectantly.

"They've just got to the Holbein—the picture called The Black Death."

"Of Judge Cremond?"

"That's right."

"Well?"

"They say it's not a Holbein at all."

17

Sloan would have given a great deal not to have been interrupted at that precise moment.

The very last thing he wanted to do at this minute was to talk to his colleague Inspector Harpe of Berebury's traffic division.

Inspector Harpe, who was known throughout the Calleshire constabulary as Happy Harry because he had never been seen to smile—he maintained that there had so far never been in anything to smile at in traffic division—had actually telephoned him at Ornum House and was asking for him urgently.

One of Sloan's own constables brought him the message. One of the first acts of the police posse from Berebury had been to take over the telephone. Another had been to encircle the house. Lady Alice Cremond would have had a phrase for that.

Stoppin' the earths.

That was what he was trying to do now. Now he had got onto the right scent at last.

Inspector Harpe soon drove all huntin', shootin', and fishin' analogies out of his mind.

"That you, Sloan?" he asked guardedly. "About this other business—you know ..."

"I know."

"There was an accident just before dinnertime today at the foot of Lockett Hill—near the bottom by the bend—you know ..."

"It's a bad corner."

"You're telling me. We've been trying to get the county council to put a better camber on it for years, but you know what they're like."

"I do."

"They say it's the ministry, but then they always do."

"And the ministry say it's the county," condoled Sloan.

"That's right—how did you know? And everyone blames the police. It was a fatal, by the way."

So someone had died while "they" were fighting about improving the road.

144

"And what happened?" Sloan prompted him. Happy Harry wasn't the only one with a fatal on his hands today.

"We had this call and my nearest car was practically at Cullingoak—it couldn't have been farther away, Sloan, if it had tried."

"That's how it goes," agreed Sloan. He hadn't time to be standing here commiserating with his colleagues. "So ..."

"By the time it got from Cullingoak to Lockett Hill ..."

With blue tower light flashing, two-tone horn blaring, and every child on the route shouting encouragement.

"By the time it arrived," said Harpe, "the garage—*the* garage—if you know what I mean ..."

"I know."

"They were there."

"Damn."

"Sloan, I trust those boys. They're good lads for all that I shout at them."

"Quite, but that doesn't help, does it?" It might hinder, but Sloan didn't say so.

"They must find out some other way," insisted Harpe.

"How?" said Sloan automatically.

In a case like this it was not enough just to prove—or have events prove for you—that someone was guiltless. Oh, it might be all right in a court of law ... what was it called in England? The accusatorial system: Has this person been proved by the prosecution beyond reasonable doubt to have committed whatever it was you were accusing him of?

Or her?

But as far as he, Sloan, was concerned, give him the other approach—the Continental one—any day of the week.

The inquisitorial outlook.

Who committed the crime? Just as with Inspector Harpe's traffic division crews, so it was here at Ornum now. Events had proved that William Murton was not likely to have been guilty of the murder of Osborne Meredith, but those same events had not revealed the true sequence of events.

Yet.

"How," he repeated. "Someone must have told the garage where to go. Someone must have been telling them each time or they couldn't have been getting there so quickly."

"I know," mourned Harpe. "I've done my best. I've been reading up all those incidents ..."

Incidents was a good word.

Even in his present hurry Sloan could appreciate it. It covered every-thing from a flying bomb to an allegation of conduct unbecoming to a police officer and a ... with an effort he brought his mind back to what Happy Harry was saying.

Before he mixed his metaphors.

"And one thing struck me," went on Harpe, "as common to them all. Until now."

"Oh?" Only long training kept Sloan's ear to the telephone. He wanted so badly to throw it down and bring his mind back to Ornum.

"Each time the breakdown van got on to one of those accident jobs so mysteriously ..."

"Yes?"

"It was out of working hours. Take last night, for instance, at Tappett's Corner ..."

"But not today surely," said Sloan. "Today's Monday. Isn't it?"

He wouldn't have been unbearably surprised to learn that they had run over into Tuesday—Sunday seemed so long ago.

"That's right. Today spoils it."

"It'll have to wait," said Sloan pointedly. He would ring off in a minute and pretend afterwards that he'd lost the connection.

"I'll have to tell the Old Man," said Harpe unhappily.

"I'm afraid so."

"You don't think it'll stop him screaming for help over your business?"

"He's probably doing it already," said Sloan.

Charles Purvis took him along to the long gallery as soon as he put the telephone down.

"I'd clean forgotten about them," admitted the steward. "I never gave them another thought."

"Who are they?"

"They call themselves the Young Masters Art Society and they're do-ing a European picture tour taking in as many ..."

"Old Masters?"

"That's right. As many Old Masters as they can. They've already done one trip doing the public collections, galleries, and so forth."

"It's not the same," said Sloan promptly. If he had learned anything from his twenty-four hours in Ornum House it was that.

"No," agreed Charles Purvis. "That's what they say."

They went back up the stairs, Constable Crosby two paces behind them.

"I was just taking them round the long gallery," went on Purvis, "tell-ing them what little I did know about the pictures—it's not very much actually because that's not my line. I'd told them about Mr. Meredith, though, and explained that they'd have to make do with me when we got round to the Holbein."

"Halfway down on the right-hand wall in a bad light?"

"That's right. It doesn't do to put your best picture in full sunlight." Charles Purvis might not know as much about the paintings as Osborne Meredith, but he had been trained in how to care for them. "You keep it away from daylight as much as you can. Certain sorts of artificial lights are better …"

Inspector Sloan halted suddenly on the staircase.

Constable Crosby didn't and all but cannoned into him from behind and below.

"Miss Cleepe." cried Sloan, bringing his hand down on the banister in a great smack. "She told us this morning …"

"Miss Cleepe?" Purvis merely looked bewildered. "Miss Cleepe didn't tell us anything."

"A walloping great clue," declared Sloan solemnly, "and we none of us spotted it. Did we?"

"No, sir," said Constable Crosby.

"No, Inspector," said Purvis wonderingly. "Miss Cleepe? Are you sure you mean Miss Cleepe?"

"Miss Cleepe. Crosby, it's in your book what she said."

Crosby obediently turned back the pages in his notebook, licking his thumb as he did so. "Would it be the bit about the Holbein, sir?"

"Of course it's about the Holbein," snapped Sloan testily. "Can't you see, Crosby, that all of this is about the Holbein? It always has been. Right from the very beginning, only we didn't know."

"No, sir"—staidly. Crosby ran his finger down the page. "Where do you want me to start?"

"They were talking about the long gallery being rather dark," said Sloan, "and then Miss Cleepe said something about—"

"I've got it, sir. Here. It was after that bit about the ghost. Miss Cleepe said, 'It's such a long, narrow room, and the bulb in its own little light is broken. Dillow's getting another for me.' "

"The light over the picture was broken," breathed Purvis. "Of course."

"I should have spotted that," said Sloan. "It was a break with normality and so it was significant."

"There is this special light over the picture," agreed Purvis. "It's meant to show it up without injuring it. It doesn't get a lot of light otherwise."

Constable Crosby made a credible attempt at imitating the refined tones of Mrs. Mompson by raising his voice to an affected squeak and reading from his notebook, " 'It's practically in the half dark in the Long Gallery where it is. Halfway from each window and not very good windows at that.' "

Sloan said, "Are you feeling all right, Crosby?"

"Yes, sir. Thank you, sir."

Charles Purvis said slowly, "Someone put a broken light bulb in so people shouldn't get a good view of the picture."

"That's right."

"Most people wouldn't know the difference between the one that's hanging there and the real thing. I wouldn't for one—you'd have to be a real expert."

"We aren't concerned about most people," said Sloan, "are we? We're concerned with one person."

"Osborne Meredith."

"Precisely."

"The real expert," agreed Purvis. "The only person who would know."

"Other than The Young Masters," said Sloan softly.

"You mean they come into this, too?"

"I shouldn't be surprised."

Charles Purvis grasped the balustrade of the staircase. "This is all getting very complicated, Inspector."

"On the contrary," said Sloan. "It's getting simpler and simpler all the time. I now know what Mr. Hamilton should be looking for in the muniments room. Crosby …"

"Sir?"

"Assemble everyone in the private apartments, please, while I see The Young Masters and the archivist."

Though it was teatime there was nothing of the drawing-room tea party about the gathering in the private apartments now. True, people were drinking tea, but they were drinking it thirstily because they needed it. They were not eating at all because they were not hungry.

The only person, in fact, to touch the food, noted Sloan, had been Cousin Gertrude. With her, the shock over William Murton's death had taken a different form. She had forgotten to take off the gardening apron in which she had been doing the flowers. A pair of scissors poked out of the apron pocket and a piece of twine drooled down the front.

William Murton's death had driven the Countess to even greater heights of absentmindedness. She was pouring tea as if her life depended on it, but the hand that held the teapot shook so much that as much tea went in the saucer as in the cup. Dillow made one or two deft attempts to field the wavering stream, but in the end he went away for more hot water and clean saucers.

Mr. Adrian Cossington was very much taking a back seat, but Laura Cremond had been badly affected by the news. She was sitting—unusually docile—beside Miles on a small chiffonier. Her face had a pinched, frightened look and she never took her eyes off Inspector Sloan's face.

He and Crosby were seated near the door. If he leaned a fraction to his right, Sloan could see through the window and down to the main door of the house. There were two figures in blue standing where once footmen in powder had waited—only these two figures were policeman and their different duty was to let no one pass. There were other figures, too, at all the other exits from Ornum House, but only Sloan and Crosby knew this.

Mr. Ames had gone across to the church, otherwise everyone was in the house.

Lady Eleanor looked as if she had been crying and Lord Henry as if his hand was hurting him. Dillow came back with more hot water for the Countess.

"I knew someone was going to die what with the Judge walking and everything," said Cousin Gertrude gruffly. "Didn't think it would be William though."

"But why did it have to be William?" asked Lady Eleanor, a husky catch in her voice. "I know he was difficult and odd, but he wouldn't have really harmed anyone ..."

Inspector Sloan shuffled his notes. "I think, your Ladyship, that he came up to the house on Friday evening."

"I didn't see him."

"Nobody saw him."

"Well, then, how do you know ..."

"I don't know," said Sloan, "but I think. I think he came up quietly round about the time you were all dressing for dinner."

"Nobody much about then," grunted the Earl.

"Exactly. It's the one time when you could all be expected to be in your rooms." He paused significantly. "A fact, incidentally, also appreciated by Osborne Meredith's murderer."

There was total silence in the room. The Countess stopped pouring tea and the silver teapot hovered, precariously suspended over a cup. Dillow was going to be lucky to escape scalding.

"But why did he come up like that in the first place?" Lord Henry wanted to know. "He was always welcome, you know. He wasn't as bad a chap as you might think from talking to him. Didn't do himself justice."

"He might," said Sloan cautiously, "have been in the habit—the bad habit—of coming up here without any of you knowing."

The Earl cleared his throat. "Very true, Inspector. I think he did. Suspected it myself before now."

"Harry!" That was the Countess. "You never told me."

"No need, my dear. As Eleanor says, he was quite harmless."

"But what did he do here?"

"Nothing, probably. Just have a look round."

"And where did he go?"

The Earl gave his mustache a tug. "I expect the inspector has guessed."

Sloan nodded. "I think so, my lord. I think William Murton was in the habit—the bad habit—of slipping up into the room behind the peephole."

"To see what he could see," said Lord Henry slowly.

Sloan turned. "Yes, my lord. Somebody watched me from there this morning, but when I got up to the room they'd gone."

"Not William surely?"

"No," said Sloan. "That was somebody else watching me." Now he knew who that had been, too. There had been two people in the vicinity to choose from.

"William saw something on Friday," concluded Lady Eleanor shakily.

"Something nasty," put in Cousin Gertrude, winding twine round her finger.

"Something very nasty," agreed Sloan. "I think he saw someone carrying the body of Osborne Meredith across the great hall to the armory staircase."

"How very clever," observed the Countess inconsequentially.

Her husband turned. "Clever, m'dear?"

"To choose the only time when we would none of us be about." She smiled sweetly. "That means it must be someone who knows us really well, doesn't it?"

Perhaps, thought Sloan, one could redefine an aristocrat as a man or woman to whom a fact held no terror.

"I think," murmured the Earl, "we are already agreed on that."

"It stands to reason anyway," said Cousin Gertrude, that firmly entrenched spinster, who, having long ago abandoned feeling, was left only with logic.

Over on the chiffonier Laura Cremond stirred. "I don't know how you can all just sit here without knowing."

"Difficult, what?" agreed Miles.

"Perhaps," said Lord Henry acutely, "the inspector wants a little suspense."

What, in fact, Sloan was waiting for was a message from the county archivist, Mr. Robert Hamilton.

He got it quite soon.

P.C. Bloggs knocked on the door and handed him a note.

It was all he needed now.

18

Whether Sloan wanted any extra suspense or not he got it with the arrival at the door of the private apartments a moment or two later of Charles Purvis and a large genial man who introduced himself as Fortescue.

"Cromwell T. Fortescue of the Young Masters Art Society," he said, "visiting your house by courtesy of Earl Ornum to see your beautiful pictures."

The Countess seized another cup and began to pour wildly.

Charles Purvis followed him in and, noticed Sloan, maneuvered himself into a position exactly opposite Lady Eleanor. It was obvious that he had long ago learned the lesson of the lovelorn, that you can sit opposite someone without seeming to stare whereas if you sit beside them you have to keep turning your head.

Which is noticeable.

The Earl grunted, "You've told him about Meredith, have you, Purvis?"

"Indeed, he has, milord," responded Mr. Fortescue before Purvis could speak. "I am deeply sorry. The whole of our society would wish to be associated with these sentiments, I know."

"A message has arrived from Miss Meredith, too," said Charles Purvis. "She's seen an early edition of an evening paper and she's coming back straightaway."

"Poor dear," said the Countess. "Charles, will you meet her at the station and see that she doesn't need anything? She might like to come up here for the night."

Sloan doubted it, but did not say so. In Miss Meredith's position he'd have opted for his own little house, where you could at least count the rooms.

"We'll have to see about the vault, too," said the Earl.

Death might be the great leveller, noted Sloan silently, but William Murton was wholly family now.

Cromwell T. Fortescue wasn't used to being overlooked. He said loudly and clearly, "We're sorry to have arrived at a time like this, my lord ..."

The Earl inclined his head.

"And also to be the bearers of such sad news, but Cyrus Phillimore is quite sure of his facts."

"More bad news?" said Laura Cremond faintly. "I don't believe it. There can't be any more."

"It may not be news, of course," said Fortescue more tentatively, "but I hardly think the Earl here would subscribe to a deception."

"Certainly not," said Adrian Cossington, the solicitor, upon the instant, "and should you be inferring this ..."

"What," asked the Earl of Ornum mildly, "is Mr. Fortescue trying to tell us?"

"Among your paintings, Earl," said Mr. Fortescue, "you have a painting said to be by Hans Holbein the Younger."

"We have."

"It's one of the lesser-known ones because it's been here since he painted it. One owner, you might say."

"That is so. My ancestor, the Judge, had it painted in 1532, the year before ... before the family tragedy. Holbein was in London then ... just beginning to make his name."

"Cyrus Phillimore agrees with all that," said Fortescue. "The only thing he doesn't agree with is that Holbein painted this particular picture. He says it's a fake." Dillow pressed a cup and saucer into his hand and the courtly Mr. Fortescue bowed in the direction of the Countess. "I guess it's not the sort of news that any of you wanted to hear ..."

The Countess hadn't yet remembered to put the teapot back on the tray, but it didn't stop her talking.

"Tell me, Mr. Fortescue, how long hasn't it been a Holbein?"

"I couldn't begin to tell you that, Countess. Only that Cyrus Phillimore says ..."

Lord Henry said quietly, "Not very long, Mother." He turned slightly. "That right, Inspector?"

"Yes, my lord. Not very long."

"Friday?" suggested Lord Henry.

"Very possibly, my lord."

"Friday afternoon perhaps ..."

"Perhaps, my lord."

"Ossy's discovery!" cried Lady Eleanor. "That must have been what Ossy discovered! That the Holbein was a fake."

"We think so, your Ladyship."

The Countess of Ornum lowered the teapot onto the large silver tray with a clatter. "You mean the picture was actually changed over on Friday afternoon?"

"Yes, your Ladyship."

"And that little Mr. Meredith knew about the change?"

"We think he spotted it by accident."

Cromwell T. Fortescue began, "Cyrus Phillimore says it's a very good fake …"

Nobody took any notice of him.

"And having spotted it," said Lord Henry, "he dashed to the telephone to ring up his pal the vicar to ask him to pop along and confirm his worst suspicions."

"That's what we think, my lord," agreed Sloan. "It would be the natural thing to do before he told your father. After all, it is a pretty serious allegation."

"I'll say," said his young Lordship inelegantly. "He's worth a pretty packet is the old Judge."

"And where is he now?" demanded Cousin Gertrude.

Laura Cremond said unsteadily, "I know where the picture is."

Everyone looked towards the sharp-faced woman who sat beside Miles.

"I say," said Miles. "Do you? Good."

She ignored him. "It's lying under a pile of old maps in the muniments room. It's not damaged at all."

There was an expectant silence.

"I'm afraid," went on Laura Cremond, not without dignity, "that I have a confession to make, and it's very kind of the inspector to give me the chance."

Miles looked as if he couldn't believe his eyes and ears. "I say, old girl, steady on. This isn't a revivalist meeting, you know."

"I'm sorry to have to tell you," said Laura, "that on Friday evening I behaved rather badly."

"Not as badly as somebody else," said the Countess sadly.

"Nearly," insisted Laura. "I'm afraid I disturbed the muniments."

"Good Lord!" said Miles.

"I'm very sorry. I just couldn't bear the thought of Uncle Harry not being Earl any more."

Cousin Gertrude had finished winding up the twine. "If Laura saw it there," she said bluntly, "why didn't she tell us and save all this trouble?"

Laura flushed and her voice was so low as to be nearly inaudible. "I didn't like to say …"

"You didn't like to say!" exclaimed Cousin Gertrude scornfully; Gertrude, who had herself never left anything unsaid.

"I thought perhaps Uncle Harry had arranged to …" Laura faltered and began again. "Owners do change pictures over themselves sometimes, you know, and sell the original without saying anything to anyone."

"I expect," murmured the Countess serenely, "he will one day."

Laura was getting to her feet. "I know I did something I shouldn't, Uncle Harry and Aunt Millicent, and I'm very sorry. Miles and I are going now and we shan't be expecting any more invitations to stay at Ornum."

The Earl was keeping to a more important train of thought. "So Meredith was killed because he knew about the fake picture."

"And to prevent him telling anyone else, my lord." A steel-like quality crept into Sloan's voice. He cleared his throat and everyone turned in his direction. If you cleared your throat in the Berebury Police Station they thought you had a cold coming, but it was different here.

Everything was different here.

"It all happened," he said, "because he wasn't invited to tea with your Lordship's aunts like he usually was on Fridays."

"You're joking, Inspector," Gertrude Cremond said.

"Indeed I'm not, madam. I'm perfectly serious. As a rule Mr. Osborne Meredith always took tea with their Ladyships upstairs on Fridays."

"You could count on it," said Lady Eleanor.

"Someone did," said Sloan soberly, "and it was his undoing."

The Countess of Ornum picked up the teapot again. Dillow peered into the hot-water jug and, apparently finding it empty, picked it up.

"Don't go, Dillow."

"Very well, sir." He stood with the jug in his hand.

"Friday," said Sloan, "was an exception. Their Ladyships upstairs did not invite Mr. Meredith to tea as he had offended them by his historical researches. They did not, however, tell anyone they hadn't done so."

"So poor old Ossy turns up in the long gallery just after the Holbein had been changed over," concluded Lord Henry, "when by right he should have been pinned between Great Aunt Alice and Great Aunt Maude while they told him how things ain't what they used to be."

"Quite so."

"Then what, Inspector?"

"Then," said Sloan in a voice devoid of emphasis, "he goes to the telephone where he is overheard ringing the vicar's wife." He turned towards Lord Ornum. "Your telephone isn't exactly private, your Lordship."

"It's the draftiest place in the house," responded the Earl. "My father wouldn't have it anywhere else. Didn't like it."

"After that," said Sloan, "I reckon the murderer had about a quarter of an hour in hand. A quarter of an hour in which to decide what to do and to go down to the armory and pick his weapon."

Lady Eleanor shivered. "If only I'd stayed talking to Ossy ..."

"No, your Ladyship, that wouldn't have made any difference. He'd have just waited until you'd gone."

A thought had penetrated Miles Cremond's brain. "I say, Inspector, you couldn't go walking through the house with a club, what? Look very odd."

"Yes, sir, I quite agree. There is one way though in which it could be carried quite easily without being seen."

Miles Cremond, having had one thought, wasn't immediately up to another. He frowned, but said nothing.

"And don't forget," went on Sloan smoothly, "that Mr. Meredith wouldn't have known who to suspect of changing the picture. Dillow, I think her Ladyship has finished with the tea tray now. Would you like to take it away?"

"Certainly, sir." With an expressionless face the butler put the hot-water jug back beside the teapot and picked up the tray.

He was halfway across the room with it when Sloan said to him conversationally, "Did you have any trouble hiding the godentag under Mr. Meredith's tea tray, Dillow?"

In the end it wasn't the Countess of Ornum at all who dropped the silver teapot.

It was Dillow.

"That you, Sloan?" Superintendent Leeyes didn't wait for an answer. "I think it's high time we got some help in this case."

"There's no need now, sir, thank you."

"Can't have the Earl thinking we aren't efficient. I'm going to ring the chief constable now and tell him that—"

"I've just made an arrest, sir."

"I think we should ask him to call in Scotland Yard. After all, you've had nearly twenty-four hours and—"

"I've just arrested Michael Joseph Dillow, sir."

"Who?"

"The butler."

"What for?"

"The murder of Osborne Meredith."

"Are you sure?"

"Yes, sir. It all fits in."

"What does?"

"Motive, means, opportunity ..." Sloan couldn't think offhand what else constituted a murder case.

"Motive?"

"Theft, sir. Of a very valuable picture. I think," added Sloan judiciously, "that he had a bit of really bad luck there."

"Where?"

"In Osborne Meredith spotting the switchover just when he did."

"So"—astringently—"did Meredith."

"Quite so, sir. Otherwise Dillow had timed things quite well. Meredith was sure to be at the two-day cricket match on the Saturday and Sunday—he would never have missed that if he was alive—and it was highly unlikely that anyone but Meredith would have spotted that the Holbein was a fake. The forgery's a really expert job."

"Who did it?"

"Dillow won't tell us, but I strongly suspect that same hand that did the pseudo Van Goghs which his last employer found he owned."

Superintendent Leeyes grunted.

"But to lessen the risk," pursued Sloan, "Dillow put a dud electric light bulb in the fitting over the picture. It's in a bad light as it is and Miss Cleepe is short-sighted anyway and isn't an expert."

"Then what?" demanded Leeyes.

"I think he killed him when he took his tea tray in, ate the tea himself, and left the body in the library."

"Sloan"—irritably—"there's something very old-fashioned about all this—butlers and bodies in the library."

"Traditional, sir," Sloan reminded him. "You said we could expect the traditional at Ornum."

Leeyes grunted again.

"He left him in the library, sir, while he deflected the vicar. It's not the sort of library anyone uses much in the ordinary way. Then after he sounded the dressing bell—the only dressing bell Sloan knew was that on his own alarm clock, which went off every morning at seven o'clock, not every evening at seven-thirty, but he was prepared to believe that there were others—"while all those in the house were changing he carried the body down to the armory."

"Quite a good time to choose."

"Very. Except for one thing. William Murton was watching him from the spyhole above the great hall. As well as seeing Dillow carrying Mr. Meredith's body he also saw the chandelier lying on the table—which was what put us on to him having been there." Sloan discreetly omitted Lady Alice from the narrative. Ghosts were all very well in Ornum House: in the stark, scrubbed police office in Berebury they became too insubstantial to mention.

"What put you on to Dillow?" enquired Leeyes. "That's more important."

"Teacups," said Sloan. "There should have been three on their Lady-ships' tray."

"Teacups?"

"There were only two," explained Sloan, "which meant that by the time he took them their tea Dillow must have already overheard Meredith telling the vicar's wife that he would be waiting for her husband in the library and guessed exactly what discovery Meredith had made."

"Meredith could have told him himself that he wasn't going up to the two old birds," objected Leeyes.

"If he did, sir, then Dillow was lying when he said he hadn't seen him earlier. Six of one, half a dozen of the other."

"And Murton?"

"William Murton decided that in future Dillow could subsidize his plea-sures—he therefore didn't ask his uncle for a loan this weekend—which I gather was something so unusual as to be remarkable."

"So he got what was coming to him."

"I'm afraid so, sir. As soon as he tried it on, probably. He was deal-ing with a tougher nut than he knew. Than we knew," Sloan added honestly. Dillow hadn't gone quietly, but there had been policemen everywhere.

"Hrrrrrrmph," said Leeyes. "And what stopped Dillow just clearing off with the picture?"

"Michael Fisher, Mrs. Laura Cremond, and me," said Sloan. "The boy found Mr. Meredith too soon, Mrs. Cremond stirred up the muniments, and I sealed the door. If I hadn't I think it would have gone out today under Dillow's arm."

"Today?"

"His day off. Bad luck, really. He parked it in the safest place he knew. He tried to break the door down in the night and to lure the archivist out with food today."

"Hrrrrrrmph," said Leeyes again. "And Murton?"

"I expect," said Sloan, "Dillow suggested he and Murton go some-where for a nice quiet chat—like the dungeons."

Inspector Sloan had left Constable Crosby and Constable Bloggs on duty outside the door of the private apartments with firm instructions about the Ornum family remaining undisturbed.

The door, therefore, in theory should not have opened at all at this juncture, still less should an incredibly old lady in black have got past them armed with nothing more intimidating than a lorgnette.

But she had.

"Why," demanded the querulous voice of Lady Alice Cremond, "has Dillow not brought us our tea?"

Detective Constable Crosby turned the police car in that wide sweep of carriageway in front of Ornum House where the coaches of the Earls of Ornum had been wont to go into that wide arc of drive that brought them to the front door.

There was room to have paraded the entire County of Calleshire Force and to spare but there were only two members of it present: Inspector Sloan and Constable Crosby.

"Home, James, and don't spare the horses," commanded Sloan, climbing in.

"Beg pardon, sir?"

Sloan sighed. "Headquarters, Crosby, please."

"Yes, sir."

They drove through the park, past the folly, ignoring the Earl's prize deer. Crosby steered the car between the gryphons on the gate finial without a sidelong glance.

Sloan looked at his watch and thought that—with a bit of luck—he'd be home in time to nip round his garden before the light went. Yesterday—was it only yesterday?—there had been a rose—new rose—nearly out. It might not be good enough for showing, but he thought he would try.

You could never tell with judges.

They left the copybook village of Ornum behind and got on the open road.

They were on the outskirts of Berebury when they saw the ambulance.

It was in a hurry. Crosby slowed down and eased to the side of the road as it flashed by in the opposite direction. The sound of its siren was nearly extinguished by the roar of the motorcycle that was following the ambulance at great speed.

"That's Pete Bellamy, that is," observed Crosby inconsequentially.

"Well I hope traffic pick him up."

"Always follows the blood wagon, does Pete."

"Say that again, Crosby."

"About Pete Bellamy, sir? He lives opposite the ambulance station."

"Where does he work?"

"Some garage in the town, sir. He's just got himself the bike."

"So that each time the bell goes down he chases the ambulance."

"That's right."

"Only when he's not at work of course."

"That's right, sir."

"What's his dinnertime?"

"I couldn't say, sir. It is important?"

"And if it's a smashup he rings his boss."

"I expect so, sir. They don't pay them a lot you know. Not apprentices."

"And his boss comes out with the breakdown truck on the off chance."

"They do it in other places," said Crosby defensively. "Big mainroad counties. Near black spots and so forth. The truck just follows the ambulance."

"Maternity cases," said Sloan sarcastically, "must be a big disappointment to them."

"It's probably worth it," said Crosby. "One good roundabout's worth a lot of swings in the car trade." He said anxiously, "Is it important, sir? Shall I have to tell him to stop?"

Sloan breathed very deeply. "No, Crosby. Just to drive more carefully."

He reached into his briefcase for the formal charge sheet.

Presently he read it out to a sullen silent prisoner.

"Michael Joseph Dillow you are charged that on Friday, June 20, last, you did feloniously cause the death of one Osborne Meredith, against the Peace of Our Sovereign Lady the Queen, her Crown and Dignity …"

Sloan paused.

He hadn't thought of it like that before either.

THE END